PEOPLE OF THE VALLEY

OTHER BOOKS BY FRANK WATERS

Midas of the Rockies (1937)
The Man Who Killed the Deer (1942)
The Colorado (1946)
The Yogi of Cockroach Court (1947)
Masked Gods: Navajo and Pueblo
   Ceremonialism (1950)
The Earp Brothers of Tombstone (1960)
Book of the Hopi (1963)
Leon Gaspard (1964)
The Woman at Otowi Crossing (1966)
Pumpkin Seed Point (1969)
Pike's Peak (1971)

PEOPLE OF THE VALLEY

FRANK WATERS

THE **SWALLOW PRESS** INC.
CHICAGO

Sage Books are published by
The Swallow Press Incorporated
1139 South Wabash Avenue
Chicago, Illinois 60605

This book is printed on 100% recycled paper.

ISBN (clothbound edition) 0-8040-0242-8
ISBN (paperbound edition) 0-8040-0243-6
Library of Congress Catalog Card Number 78-137435

To the people of the beautiful blue
valley, and to those who have loved it:
Gente muy remota, muy cerrada—
amigos bien recordados, muy cariñosos.

PEOPLE OF THE VALLEY

1

To three races and four generations, through all its many names, it has been known simply as the beautiful blue valley. It is not as beautiful as it is blue. Nor always blue. Yet the tone persists when the vegas turn sere and tawny under drought, and the pine slopes white with frost. And seen from above the haze of Indian summer and the winter mists, from the top of the nine thousand foot pass, the valley appears always what it is—a crescent lake of blue draining the shadows of the steep-walled cañons which hem it on all sides.

It drains more than shadows and the shadows of the men with a wild remoteness in their eyes. A thunder cloud snags on the western cliffs of the Sangre de Cristo, and from the converging box cañons of Luna and Lujan the water foams down along the ridge rock of Los Alamitos. The trout stream at Guadalupita swells from a rain in the north, and rises higher at Turquillo from the drainage of La Cañada de Carro. Melting snows rush down the glacial bed of Rio de la Casa, swamping the beaver dams. To the east and south the Coyote and Cebollita overflow the pastures, the fields and valleys of the Big Onion and the Little.

And the tiny river no longer meanders, poco a poco, through the beautiful blue valley. It rips through the willows, uproots cottonwoods, tears out old acequias so patiently banked by hand. The chalk cliffs crumble; the rutty roads dissolve into rivers of slimy glue; corn milpas look like muddy rice fields. Dead chickens are cast up on the beaches of flooded corrals. A drowned calf, neck broken, hangs over a patch of fence. Adobes wash out too, crumbling back into the earth from which they rose and will stubbornly rise again.

Each swollen tributary, in turn, marks the seasons, alters the landscape if only by a foot, and brings crops and people God's blessing or the devil's own.

But sometimes a cloudburst up one of the cañons marks the year as one of many to be remembered. The decades are labeled by such washouts. And the people divide their lives by what has happened once.

Twenty or thirty years it has made. Quien sabe? It was the flood. A cloudburst. It broke on the ridge and poured down both cañons at once. Two. Not one. Two, Señores. Madre de Dios! The water! How it came! Here to my very feet it rose. Verdad! From El Alto de Talco to El Alto de los Herreras, from Cañoncito to La Cueva, the valley was one lake. The floor of the church was wet when we heard mass. Santísima! That's how it was.

So now they are building a dam.

Who?

They. El Estado. The Governor. The políticos for whom we made crosses on our votes, as instructed. Perhaps the Presidente himself. . . . Who knows these things exactly when he is busy in the fields?

What dam?

Burro! Fool! The dam so that we won't have any more floods. Across the valley, at the mouth of the cañon.

But I don't see any dam. What kind of a dam is it that a man cannot see? Forgive me, friend, but I am of the people; I do not understand. But I don't see any dam. No, certainly, I can see nothing there but that fence which Fulgencio Garcia y Valdes should have fixed when I told him about his two cows in my oats. And that old mare, too, the one with the evil eye. . . .

Sacred Heart of Jesus! There is no dam! But they are building it just the same. On paper first, as is the way nowadays. A big dam. A dirt dam. A check dam.

Oh sí! Sí. Sí, Señor. A dam de checks! Of course. Of course. There must be many checks—to pay us for hay for their horses, for adobes, for work perhaps. I have seen in the store such checks. Little pieces of paper good for money. We shall all be rich. . . . But still, amigo, why do they build this dam? There has never been one before; it is not the custom. The floods come, like sunshine and the drought. They are all God's will. Else why should there be floods? No doubt it is wrong to stop them. No; I do not see why there should be a dam. Why should there be a dam, Señor?

It is explained to everyone, there in the sloping campo where even the pines march down to listen, soughing among themselves like the echoed whisper of the multitude.

The wary, flint-eyed men who have ridden out of the dark mountain fastness of Las Colonias and El Quemado still sit their restless mounts, swaying like reeds in the breeze. Families and neighbors who have bumped since sunrise over the rocky roads from Vallecito and Lucero squat patiently in the crowded box wagons. Barefoot women and ragged men who have plodded down the trails from west, north, east and south; from El Alto with brown faces tinged red from Indian Picuris; villagers, shopkeepers, strangers—all, mouths agape, huddle under sun and dust and flies.

Of course it is a fiesta. Only a fiesta could bring them together. Since yesterday afternoon the long barbecue trench has been fed till it is two feet deep with glowing coals. Four steers, two sheep and three pigs have been basted with a mess of brown sugar, vinegar, black and cayenne pepper, tomato paste, salt and chile; have been cut into chunks, and wolfed down with bread and one hundred and fifty pounds of potato and onion salad. Now, with something solid in the belly to counteract the unusual stimulus of mind and spirit, they stare fixedly at the platform in front—the back of a truck covered with planks and hung with an American flag.

There are many speeches and many speakers. Flowery speeches from local políticos for whom the little crude crosses were marked on the votes, and demanded. Long speeches from city Anglos properly sweating in white collars and buttoned coats. Speeches crisp and awesome with facts and figures from visiting ingenieros who are building the dam on paper, first.

Such a big dam to be built on paper! Where does it all come from, this paper?

A thunderbolt sentence, a flowery phrase. An outflung arm, a pause. The speaker spits out dust, runs a forefinger under his limp collar. The interpreter beside him duly translates.

So it goes on all afternoon.

The dam looms up, bigger, clearer. Here, in this valley. There, at the mouth of the cañon. So long, so wide, so high. And there will be a lake behind. Imagine, a lake! Strange. There has never been a lake here before. It is not the custom. And a new road, a slick shiny road. Many automobiles will come whizzing by where one chugged, bogged down and was dragged out by teams before.

Progress is coming to the beautiful blue valley. It sounds muy importante. The people are properly impressed.

El Estado, the Governor, the políticos for whom they made the tiny crosses as instructed, the Presidente himself—how is it that all these should be so good, so generous, so truly thoughtful of the people of the lonely valley so long forgotten in the mountains? Pues, the dam! they are going to build a dam. Like the one on paper.

But what is this? A rippling tenseness draws the crowd together. The dam must have many varas of land. The lake must have land. Also there must be room for the road to run through the fields. Whose land? Our land. Don Teodosio's land, Maria del Valle's land, and the land of Refugio Montes and of Gertrudes Paiz . . . everybody's land perhaps. That, compadres, is a horse of a different color! We have never sold our land. It is not the custom. The land is our mother. It had suckled our fathers, our father's fathers. What would we do without land? Even with a dam?

Up on the platform somebody slyly kicks the speaker on the heel. "Sssht! Easy on that now. It isn't time." He stops with a flowery phrase.

The last speaker rises unsteadily. He is a little drunk. His straw hat sits on half his head. His bow tie jerks up and down over his Adam's apple. He brushes the interpreter aside with lordly grace.

"Caballos and Caballoses!" he shouts. "Yo pienso que si . . . que es pretty good por la public waino for maka this dam aqui!" He totters, regains his legs and flings out his arms. "Caballos and Caballoses! Muchas gracias!"

They catch him, behind by the coattails, and slide a chair under him just in time. He sits there, eyes glazed with incomprehension, before the shouting throng.

It is the best speech of the day. The inarticulate good will of drunkenness is something understood by all. But ground has been broken for the dam.

It is the crepusculo vespertino. The green of oats and wheat and corn, of pine and spruce and piñon, has lost its yellow component, but still retains its blue. The indigo shadows are not yet black. It is the blue hour between yellow sunset and black night. The bell of the village church strikes it with a faint silvery chime.

On top of a ridge above the valley a box wagon halts in the rutted road. It is loaded with people returning from the fiesta. On the plank seat rattles a little bag of bones. The bag is a pair of stained trousers with the fly unbuttoned, a rusty coat and a little black hat. Out of it protrudes two splintered bones gloved in dry yellow skin and holding the limp reins. Beside it, stiffly upright in imperious silence, sits a woman older still. The rest of the crowd squat patiently on the floor behind: thin, barefooted women huddled in black cotton rebozos, men rolling cigarettes in paper less brown than their stubby fingers, and children sleepily nodding at a dog, tongue out, which has been plodding behind.

They cross themselves, hearing the church bell, and look back down into the valley. The barbecue pit is still faintly smoking, adding blue to blue. The village lamps are coming on. In front of La Cantina Palomita is a dark crowd drinking, smoking, spitting into the street, and discussing the day's speeches.

"Of course," observes a man in the wagon. "Before the baile tonight there will be much talk. It is necessary. Perhaps we should have stayed."

But his wife sees him wet his lips. "For what?" she asks. "To get drunk and have your throat cut for nothing?"

"It is a great thing, perhaps, this dam," ventures another. "But who knows what to think? Who shall tell us?"

They look up, warily expectant, at the old woman in front. Her stiff straight back does not unbend. She maintains her imperious silence. Suddenly out of her dusty rebozo a sharp elbow strikes the bag of bones beside her.

The little black hat rears up. The skeleton hands slap the gaunt carcasses with the limp reins. It shouts. "Andale! For the love of God! Have you no breath? We shall be late with the milking."

The scrawny team plods forward. The mongrel, behind, opens his mouth and starts a long pink pendulum to swinging, like a clock jolted to sudden life. Then he trots to his post under the rear axle. And the wagon load of people dips down the rocky road into the shadows of the pines.

The silence is thick and heavy, a little triste and holding the wild remoteness of the dark, narrow cañon. It is a flood which washes up to and around the plodding horses, the panting dog and creaking wagon. The upright old woman holds it at bay with a greater silence.

Three little wooden crosses beside the road are passed. An adobe. The pale yellow lamp in the window stares after the wagon. A dog barks and is choked by the silence. Then looms a scatter of six or seven steep-roofed adobes, aspen corrals and anthill ovens—a village, as villages are in these remote cañons.

Past it the road turns right, curves upward again. A trail leads tangent through a steep corn milpa amongst the forest. The wagon stops.

The clothed skeleton on the front seat rattles with a threat of clambering down. "I shall go with you to your house, Madre," it squeaks politely. "I will see that everything is all right before I return."

The upright old woman has already got down, a little stiffly, and jangling the singletree. She wraps her rebozo about her shoulders. "Fool! Since when has Maria del Valle required the help of a man she has suckled like the sick pig of a litter?"

The skeleton sinks back with a sigh of relief into the same comfortable heap. "It is as you say, Madre."

A match flaring up in the wagon box lights the old woman's dark, wrinkled face. Its powerful and primitive features, timeless with sorrow and fecundity, are savage and enduring as if cut out of rock: a rock beaten, smashed and worn by waves but still jutting the promontory beak of nose, high cheekbones and solid jaw into the surge of life. The eyes are small and black and bright, the eyes of a hawk. Only the dark, red-brown flesh of her seamed and sagging cheeks appears touched and worn by time—but still timeless and enduring as the red-brown earth forever furrowed by the plow. She has one tooth. It is clamped down on the stub of a cigarette protruding stiffly from her loose, parted lips.

She suddenly, imperiously, reaches forth and grabs the match to light her own stub.

"A thousand pardons, Señora! I did not see. . . . Go with God, Señora."

"Yes, Yes. Adiós! Adiós, Doña Maria!"

"Muchísimas gracias! It has been a great fiesta. Buenas noches, Madre."

Abruptly, before she throws away the match, a man leans out of the wagon and asks quietly, very politely, "The dam, Doña Maria. It is too great a problem for my simple soul. The many speeches confuse me. It is good, this dam, Señora? I. . ."

The old woman lifts the match, peers forward. A low rumble from deep in her throat rises to meet a thin watery hiss in her powerful, jutting nose. Her loose wrinkled lips draw back. She spits vindictively upon the ground a vigorous expuition of great contempt. Then suddenly the match is out, the corn is rustling, and the old woman is stalking sturdily upright through the darkness.

"Ándale! For the love of God! Have you no strength? We are late with the milking."

The wagon crawls on, squeaking.

Soon in the darkness a voice speaks softly. "The Señora doesn't think well of the dam, perhaps."

"Pues. Doña Maria perhaps does not like the dam."

"Don Teodosio! Hey there, amigo! Is it possible, perhaps, that the Madre doesn't like the dam? What do you say, compadre?"

The bag of bones straightens up a bit on the seat. "I have a cigarette rolled these many minutes. But no match. Who has a match? I want to light my cigarette. But I have no match. Not in this pocket, nor in this . . . ."

Hurriedly, respectfully, a commotion produces a match.

Don Teodosio lights his cigarette. The little flame lights up half his thin, wrinkled face with its expression of cunning indolence. The other half, doubtless, is no better. He puffs a time or two. Now, a little self-conscious with authority, he says, "No. Of course. It is possible that Doña Maria does not like the dam. Who knows? But I think it is possible the Señora doesn't like the dam."

The wagon creaks on. The people nod to themselves in darkness.

It is possible that Doña Maria really doesn't like the dam.

Mid-November it is, and the Saint's Day of the village. The late morning stillness of the deserted fields is broken by a faint wailing chant. A thousand crows, polished like ebony, flap up cawing from the tawny stubble. A lone mallard shoots like an arrow from the marsh. A shaggy stallion wheels from his mares, flings up his head and stares over the fence.

The chanting wails louder. It comes from twenty men in a column of twos crossing the fields from El Alto de los Herreras. Their boots are muddy, their denim trousers ragged, but they wear neckties and wrinkled Sunday coats. All are bareheaded. Their eyes are raised to a banner of red silk lettered with faded gold. It flaps between two poles which the men in front are carrying.

As the column crosses the creek by the old mill and enters the village, the wail rises higher and falls lower. A red rooster flees squawking. A wagon draws aside to let the men pass. Clutching their rebozos to be sure their heads are covered, a few hurrying women fall in behind the column.

All cross the little plaza behind the general store. Beyond the rows of empty wagons and tethered horses the bell of the church is ringing. The tall poles dip, and the red banner slides through the adobe arch of the courtyard wall. The chanting ceases. The bell stops ringing. And in silence, down the dark nave between the cottonwoods, the people pass into the church.

Soon they come out again. The whole church empties. First the two fat, lace-robed priests. Then four men carrying on a litter Santa Gertrudes. She is almost life size, and stands swaying on a pillar in her white and dark blue robe, and wearing a manta of yellow. Her right hand carries a Bible. In her left she holds a long staff. Up it crawl two of the five mice that were carved upon it long ago when her paint was fresh and her dark cheeks not yet cracked and weathered, Behind her, head down, troop the people: humble women wrapped in their black rebozos, squat muscular men carrying their battered Stetsons, and children squeaking in new shoes. And in the rear, carrying their faded red banner, the twenty chanting men from El Alto.

The procession straggles up the one dusty road of the village, crosses the creek and winds back to the church through the scatter of log corrals and squalid adobes.

Santa Gertrudes, whose gentleness befriends even the timid mice, has blessed village and people again, and sanctified another year.

Now the people in knotted strings line the church wall, the sides of store and cantina, the courtyard and the plaza. They gossip, gesticulate, roll cigarettes. But warily, a little furtively, they watch an old woman sitting imperiously upright on the seat of a rattletrap buggy in the middle of the plaza.

Santa Gertrudes comes out once each year into her name-village with her gentle cracked smile, her mice and mercy. Already she is being stuffed away, forgotten, in her gloomy niche.

But Doña Maria has appeared for the second time with her vindictive lips drawn tight, squeezing as usual the life out of her cigarette stub. Her dark cheeks are weathered too, but not cracked. They are hard as two seasoned piñon knots. And her small bright eyes stare coldly, contemptuously, over the crowd. Perhaps, like all dictators, she knows her people better than Santa Gertrudes their transient regard for gentleness and mercy, and their enduring respect for tyranny. So she sits, straight as a pine, and as if oblivious of their sly attention. A tattered queen in a topless chariot whose old leather is as hard as its brittle hickory.

"Buenas días, Señora!"

"Cómo está, Doña Maria?"

"A very fine procession. Verdad!"

To their polite greetings, their fustian phrases—to themselves cringing past her, the old woman pays scant heed. Her acknowledgment to their obeisance is a shrug of her shoulders, a curt nod.

One of the priests comes out. He has doffed his lace and locked the church. As he waddles across the plaza the people rake off hats to hold against their breasts, bend their knees, shove children forward for his greetings. He comes abreast of the rattletrap buggy, pauses.

"Ah! Doña Maria! A splendid mass this morning! You did not come? But God still waits for you. It is never too late, Señora. Even after forty years."

Doña Maria shrugs wearily without bothering to turn around, as if more bored at his pleas than at his former maledictions. But when he has passed on, his plump face red as an apple above his stiff collar, she stares triumphantly at the crowd. Her reward is their embarrassment.

They nod slyly, poke each other in the ribs, gaze away and whisper, "You saw? She is not afraid of the Father. Of God or the devil either! What do you say now?"

They move about now in the morning sunshine, greeting friends, gossiping, begging tobacco, offering a swig of cheap whisky or a taste of stale beer—satellites swarming around a common sun, but at a respectful distance lest they be scorched.

Along the courtyard wall lounges a group of men. Another rides up, dismounts and flings the reins over his horse's head. Greetings from one cañon to many others. Talk of weather, crops, people. And finally the subject common to all.

"No doubt you have heard more of this dam, compadres? Myself, I have just this day left my work for Santa

Gertrudes."

"They are building it, primo. No doubt."

"But my wife has heard that Doña Maria del Valle doesn't think much of the dam."

"Verdad!" exclaims another, looking up from his paper of punche tobacco. "It is what we have heard at Sisneros. From my primo who came to look at my new calf, from Carmen. And his wife had it from her sister at La Jara."

"The devil take these women! They sit at their pots seeing no one all day long, and yet news comes up the cañons to them on the wind . . . Jesú Cristo! Who knows what she thinks and why?"

"It is she who sits there in Don Teodosio's old buggy," says one quietly. Then slyly he adds, "Why don't you ask her, compadre?"

All smile. It is as if each has been asked to light a keg of dynamite while the others watch from safety.

The one scowls—he in homemade leather chaps who has ridden down into the valley for the first time since summer. "A witch of an old woman! Shall my life, my new cow, be cursed for my pains? Sorda hija de tal!"

"Hush! For the love of God! She has ears for the wind, Señor." Self-consciously and apprehensively, he peeks around at the old woman still waiting alone in the buggy.

Defensively now, another adds in haste, "Still, she is a wise and powerful woman. There is none who has such power with herbs. It has made years since my Pablito had the poison from yedra. She came to us quickly, being near. No medicine. Nothing she did but spit. And the boy also she made spit, spit vigorously and copiously. Mother of God, how they spit! And the poison went. 'Remember,' she said, 'when one touches a harmful weed, when one comes in contact with the evil thing, one must spit out the evil.' "

"Cristo Rey! Listen! Is it not as you have said? It came, I have heard, from old Don Teodosio himself: when the Señora was asked about the dam. True, she did not answer. But she spit. She spit as you say. Does that not make the dam evil?"

"Look! Don Teodosio! We shall call him. . . . Hola! Hey there, amigo! We are saving you a drink—a little drink, the last in our bottle."

Don Teodosio's bones rattle in their stained trousers and rusty coat; his fly is still unbuttoned. He stops in front of the group, takes off his little black hat and brushes back his thin white hair before replacing it.

"Sit down. Among friends. In the sunshine. Ah! And here is the bottle!"

Don Teodosio watches a broad brown hand wrap around the bottleneck, as if around a rooster's throat, and yank up. He takes the opened bottle, squints at it toward the sun, then drains it at a gulp. "Hah! Fine weather, amigos! Pues!" He sinks down in a heap, props up his legs, and holds himself together with both arms.

Greetings, talk of weather, crops, people, and then. . . .

"Don Teodosio. This dam. It is too big a problem for our simple minds. We wish counsel of someone wise and learned to tell us what to think. . . . You perhaps, who have seventy years of which no more than thirty show . . . or even your esteemed mother, Doña Maria. Now if the Señora would let us know—out of her wisdom—we. . . . "

Don Teodosio has never been known to have an opinion of his own; he is liked by everyone. But his flinty brown face assumes the gravity of a priest in charge of an oracle.

"The Señora has not yet spoken. No doubt when she has consulted this year's herbs still drying . . . but already there are signs. Sí. Signs I have seen already. . . . But as I have said, there are signs. . . . "

He is arrested during his fumbling for a match by the sudden stare of Doña Maria who has just turned around in her buggy. He rises to his feet, not forgetting the proffered match, and makes off without another word.

"By all the devils of Hell!" shouts the wrinkled oracle. "Where have you been? It makes an hour I have been kept here waiting. Did I not feel my left nostril twitch? For what! To see you loafing in the sun with a bunch of lazy pigs! Get in here—old fool, sick pig of a litter. Burro!"

"Pues. Madre mia. Of course," Don Toedosio answers affably, taking up his reins. "The people are but inquiring your opinion of the dam."

"The dam. Mother of God!" The old woman leans over the side and spits, then throws back her head. And as the buggy rattles past the group of men sitting against the wall, Don Teodosio lifts his whip to them like a finger raised in admonition.

"You saw!" exclaims one, gazing after the buggy. "You saw her spit as she is said to spit each time the dam is mentioned? It is the sign."

"Sí. She is a powerful woman and wise. The time will come when she will open her heart about the dam and tell us what to think. Till then I will remember the sign equally with the talk of the políticos. 'A little shadow is worth more than a long length of sunshine.' Eh, amigos?"

The wheat has been cut, the oats, the barley. Corn has been gathered for chicos, roasted in outdoor ovens, then dried and shelled. Some has been soaked with lime to remove the husks, dried for posole or ground for nixtamal. And now the brittle stalks rustle in the wind. Rueditas, the "little wheels" of small squash have been sliced and dried. Big pumpkins have been cut round into "tasajos"—long thin strips wound up like rope and stored away. And now the withered vines glisten in moonlight with silver rime. Green chile has been roasted and peeled. Popote and popotito have been stored, and peaches, and all the herbs: cota for rheumatism, yerba del manzo for stomach pains, oshá for colds, and yerba buena to warm the insides of pregnant brides.

Time and weather have changed. Summer has gone, and all the usual crops are in. But other seeds keep growing despite the ground frosts and the snow caps eating down the mountain slopes: the seed of Doña Maria's sowing; the seeds of doubt.

She is a wise and powerful woman, and she doesn't like the dam.

2

The age of the beautiful blue valley and of Doña Maria is not, strictly speaking, a hundred years. Each is older, each echoing as they do one timeless and changeless pulse. But for a century they have been known by man—the valley ten years longer, Maria ten years less.

At the beginning of that short span six Hudson Bay trappers came warily down over the snowy pass hunting for beaver. On the banks of the frozen stream they found first three human skeletons left by Comanches, and so named the long blue crescent the valley of "L'Eau du Mort"—the Waters of the Dead.

All were Frenchmen. Roubidoux was one, and Ceran St. Vrain whose own skeleton lies yet beside the meandering stream, in the little Campo Santo rising out of the flat and covered by scrub oak. Their tongue still persists in the names of the little cañon settlements of Gascon and Ledoux, just over the hill; and it sounds at times in the general store of gruff, wooden-legged Pierre Fortier. In the church, behind, were French priests. The old linden in its courtyard, too, was a seedling brought by Father Guerin from France—one of the two which have rooted in these high western hills.

But it was up the Chihuahua Trail from Mexico, up the Rio Grande and over the Pecos, that the settlers came. Their soft fluent Spanish slurred the valley's name to "Lo de Mor," changed phonetically to "Lo de Mora," and finally shortened to "Demora." It was a place of berries, too, according to their translation: wild raspberries and strawberries thick along the streams and carpeting the clearings between thickets of chokecherry, gooseberry and wild plum. The steep, narrow cañon of Rio de la Caza, the place of the hunt, softened musically to Rio la Casa—and the beaver houses attested its change of name long after deer, wild turkey and bear grew scarce.

There were seventy-six settlers when they petitioned in the name of the Mexican nation for a land grant. Not only the long deep crescent was granted, but all the tributary cañons, the mountain uplands and the grassy plains below. And the beautiful blue valley to the north and to the south of the jutting cliffs which marked the handle of its curving bow, took two more names. The Valle de San Antonio above, and the Valle de Santa Gertrudes below.

The two villages were lifted slowly, a handful at a time, from the rich red-brown earth, roofed with vigas hand-hewn from the pines and interlaced with slim aspens. The adobes clustered thickly together for protection and according to the superior decree: "two hundred and fifty varas from East to West, leaving thirty varas outside for drippage and a common road and the meadow for the benefit of all, with its entrances and exits free."

But as the beautiful blue valley it persisted through its second name and tongue: more beautiful, more blue, as the thickets gave way to meadows of grass and the lower pine slopes to milpas of corn.

Yet little by little a third tongue, name and race crawled in. They came not over the pass from the north and west as had the first, nor up the Chihuahua Trail from the south as had the second. They came from the strange, unknown and barbaric east, over the vast buffalo plains. In great lumbering wains they came, with wheels high as a man and which left their traces forever imbedded in the soft limestone, with sheets drawn tight over the curving wagons bows—ships riding the pelagic plain. Men with eyes colder and bluer than the valley, in buckskin and with long emphatic rifles to punctuate their taciturnity. But where the wagons stopped to rest before the last climb, a fort grew up. Great walls it had, barracks and stables and courtyards where soldiers laughed, cursed, threw dice and shuffled cards. But they needed corn and wheat and oats, both men and horses—and the men wanted women and excitement.

So the beautiful blue valley over the hills prospered. For gold the village supplied liquor, gambling, horse races and cock fights. The people supplied the corn, wheat and oats for silver, and sometimes the women for a quicker exchange of lead and flashing steel. And duly, apathetically, they petitioned the new Jéfe, the Señor Presidente of the gringos, to confirm their title to their land. Again it was granted "with the stipulation that the United States herein expressly reserves to itself the buildings and improvements situated on the Fort Union Military and Timber Reservation, together with the possession and use of the same. . . . "

Save this, all the tributary cañons, the mountain uplands and the grassy plains below—a wilderness empire, remained theirs. But only the valley mattered.

New teams, new masters for the plow, but the land remains. The land that is mother to us all. An enduring truth that only her sons can know.

For the French disappeared with the beaver, leaving only their names and Pierre Fortier cursing and stamping his wooden leg. And soon the last of the gringo wagons passed over the trail, leaving the fort to crumble on the hillside and the colonel's grand piano to leer with a mouth of missing keys through the dusky parlor of the old inn.

Only the people remained rooted to their soil in a valley muy retirado, muy cerrado, that grew more isolated, more closed, within its mountain walls.

Through three tongues, three races and many names, then, the beautiful blue valley persisted; and yet it was but twenty years old when Doña Maria came. Old enough, but not too ripe, to be her mother.

Dawn-dusk drew the charcoal outline of a hut on the mountainside. Then the dirty gray light of day, like a soiled brush, thrust through the pines and smeared it with drabness. Its walls, waist-high, were heaped up stones chinked with adobe as were the gaping logs laid on top. The roof sagged with dirt and sprouted a growth of wild timothy.

A pig might have waddled out, but it was a woman who emerged into the clearing. She brought life and color into the drab monotone. About her bulging body she held a faded, striped, burnt-orange blanket. On her bare feet she wore sparse-beaded moccasins. Her long blue-black hair hung down around a smooth brown face slightly tinged red. The face was young but its pleasant immobility was marred by a strained expression of pain and anxiety. It was the look of a woman near childbirth, who watches for a man she knows will not return.

Without pausing she waddled across the flat stones in the stream and struggled up the trail. It rose through the gelid darkness of the pines into the pallid gray of scrub oak. Head down and breast heaving her protruding belly stretching the blanket in wrinkles across her broad hips, she climbed blindly, as if she had known it an incalculable number of ascents. Abruptly, across a face of frost-shattered granite, the path ended.

Below her the valley was rising out of a mist. She was standing on the tall weathered cliffs that jut out to separate the upper and lower halves of the one long valley so beautiful and blue. It curved like an Indian bow to left and right, as though the woman flexed it with her longing.

She looked toward the first mud clumps of Santa Gertrudes and San Antonio. Jets of pale smoke rose, adding blue to blue, but never the dust of a horse's hoofs from the plains below. Then the arrow of her gaze flew west to the wall of mountains.

She was Indian, Picuris, and the pueblo lay hidden behind the pass. Like her, others would be drawn out of its decaying, squalorous, mud-black walls to the tiny new settlements in the valley below. They would drift together to live about the hot springs, and be forgotten with the Mexican men who drew them hence. Only the faint red flush showing through the dark cheeks of their sons and grandsons would mark El Alto as different from the others—the rising end of the scale as Picuris lowered in oblivion.

But now, alone, she stood between them. It was day, and the rising sun marked her time on its dial.

She slumped down on her broad haunches, clasping her quivering belly, her face grown oily with sweat. Then with a last look over the precipice, she rose and stumbled weakly back down the trail.

The inside of the hut was growing gray with light. Its small room was windowless and without furniture save a deal table lashed together with rawhide, and a leather trunk. Patches of the dirt floor were hard and smooth and black with the goats' blood mixed in the adobe. In one corner was a small fireplace. Before it lay a straw mat and another blanket.

The woman pawed back the ashes, and blew the coals awake. In a nest of sticks she set a copper kettle, dropping fresh yerba buena into the water. From an earthen pot she drew out the last handful of parched corn and chewed a few kernels slowly. When the water boiled she drank the tea to ease the increasing pains of her pregnancy.

They kept mounting, bubbling up within her and sinking down, a geyser of cramps. She lay writhing on the sleeping mat, then rousing against the wall to wipe the sweat from her face.

A shaft of sunlight fell in the doorway and slowly revolved about the room. A blue jay screamed from a pine outside. Two magpies quarreled on the roof, dislodging a thin trickle of dirt between the smoke-stained vigas.

Shortly after noon the woman awoke from a sleep that was not a sleep. A deer was standing in the clearing outside of the door. The great petals of its ears were thrust forward, the sunlight glistened on its porous, rubber-black nose. Weakly the woman gathered up from the blanket a few dropped kernels of corn to toss outside. With the gesture the deer, stiff-legged, rose into the air and vanished with a twitch of its white tailpiece.

The woman's big body was now a volcano trying to erupt. Spasms of pain rolled her from side to side. From knots of cramps her arms and legs unraveled, twitching. Her face was no longer dark rose-brown. It was muddy orange. She chewed, as if starving, a corner of her blanket.

The tea was cold. It could not quench the fire within her. She rolled on her back and lay snorting through her wide nostrils.

After the next spasm she got up. The beaded moccasins she took off and laid away carefully in the old leather trunk. The blanket around her she removed, folded, and placed out of reach. Now barefooted, her wheat-sack body covered only by a loose, black cotton shift, she stood before the fireplace.

In the niche in the wall stood a small dusty Cristo carved out of cottonwood. It had been lacquered with the gelatinous glue of cow's horns and gypsum, painted with egg yolk and ochre, and rubbed with mutton tallow. All this had soaked into the wood leaving a dark, muddy Rembrandt-brown figure with a long sharp nose, a bitter mouth and one broken leg. It was her man's Santo. The woman propped it up and lit a candle before it. She stared at it wonderingly in the vain attempt to discern power in such an inimical form.

Then she brought out a small buckskin sack, touching with it her nose and mouth, her breasts and belly, the secret parts of her body, after which she hung it back around her throat.

Another recurrent convulsion doubled her like a felled tree. She straightened slowly, her moon face glistening with sweat, and laboriously looped over a rafter a long horsehair rope which dangled to the center of the floor.

Now began her labor.

Hands above her sagging head, she hung and pulled on the rope. What she needed and wanted were the strong hands of her man or of midwives around her waist: dragging their weight on her bulging body, slipping down from breasts to broad hips, squeezing, compressing, forcing out the new little life clamoring within her for outlet.

Instead, she hung there alone, doggedly straining in the dusky hut before the guttering candle. With one hand she prodded and pressed her belly and groin. Every few minutes fresh labor pains gripped her. Then she hung on with both hands. Her knees and feet twitched. Her hands slipped down the rope. Head down and moaning, her bare feet dragging in the dirt, she revolved more slowly, came to rest.

Little by little she hitched herself up, panting, waiting for the next spasm. The Cristo with his long sharp nose and bitter mouth looked on as if ironically amused—an amusement that yet seemed to have in it the compassion derived form severer suffering.

By midafternoon the floor beneath the woman was dark puddle of sweat. She could no longer hold herself up. She slipped down to her knees, legs outspread, and ripped off her soppy shift. Her long blue-black hair stuck to her broad back like a shadow.

Suddenly she rolled sideways upon the heap of blankets, howling. Her eyes filmed over. Her hands fought the air, fell and sought in the blankets something that was neither there or anywhere.

Time now had meaning. It hammered out its truth as if on

a great drum. The pulse beats throbbed through her and through the earth below, they shook the mountains and the evening star in its socket above. It was her time and another's too, and all to which they were bound in unbroken sequence by the one pulsing beat which echoes dreamily and powerfully through the earth of the flesh and the flesh of the earth alike.

And so it passed. . . .

They found her that evening—Two goatherds passing the hut, who heard the child's cries.

"Mother of God! It is she. The India. The woman of that stranger who ran away again to join the great wagons of the gringos. She has been here all this time . . . Cristo Rey! What a mess, this of woman bearing children . . . Señora!"

This man's name, where had he come from, would he return . . . what does one do now with such a tiny babe . . . would the Señora like some tea, a scrap of fat meat and a cold tortilla? Señora! Señora India!

To all their questions, pleas and exhortations the woman made no answer. They got out of her a wild and frightened look, a last choking gasp and one intelligible "Maria."

It was the only name she spoke, and so it became the child's. Red and tiny, it lay on the edge of the stained blanket. One minature hand was closed upon a bit of dirt. It was her birthright. Doña Maria never let it go.

Maria grew up with her goats. She was as scrawny and stringy-legged as they from scrambling up the rocky hillsides. Her hair too was long, coarse and tangled with burs and pine needles. Like theirs, her large, dark eyes could, in an instant, become wild and wary as though a pebble had been dropped into their placid depths. They were her only companions by day, her bedfellows at night. She drank their milk, ate their cheese and sometimes chewed a piece of their flesh. Their odor clung to her as if it were her own. Her life was like theirs save in one respect: she did not eat grass. At ten she was a little she-goat.

Their goatherds were two old philosophers. They kept back the mounting tide of life with a rampart of stones heaped across the narrow throat of a cañon. Behind it was an aspen fence and a roof of branches. To most of the valley below it looked like a corral. The inclosure did keep coyotes and an occasional bear from the flock at night; and interlaced with spruce branches in winter it kept out some snow and wind. But across the top of the high stone barricade gleamed a row of pale goat and sheep skulls. They were symbols of a school of thought, and its two exponents stared down between them into the valley with all the irreproachable dignity of their calling.

The older one sprouted on his long dark face a few gray chin whiskers like a he-goat's. Around his shoulders he wore a dirty sheepskin. He carried a staff and wielded it when pressed as Jove a thunderbolt. The other, scarcely over sixty, still betrayed a lingering worldliness by wearing a battered sombrero with its last tiny bell still dangling from its rim, brass earrings and leather leggings. It was obvious that he was conscious of his weakness. He kept wrinkling his seamed and weathered face as if he knew that the veneration accorded age and wisdom in men depended on thier outward mien.

These two viejos lived in a small hut in back of the corral. Maria ate with them. On stormy nights she also slept with them on the floor. It was a privilege granted her with new-born kids, an ailing ewe or a goat maimed by wild beasts. During blizzards the whole flock was let in.

The kids whimpered, the ewes blatted. When warm grease was smeared on a lacerated leg a new voice added to the bedlam and muted the shrieking winds. Maria did the smearing. She sat on the goat's head and kept ducking back from its threshing legs.

The two old men squatted in front of the fire, watching. Generously they offered tidbits of advice from their feast of wisdom. They minded neither the stench, the noise nor the gusts of smoke that filled the hut. They were immersed in life yet never wetted; salved too, as it were, by the protective goose grease of their inherent aloofness.

Both had come up from the desert wastes of Chihuahua. The lush grass and innumerable streams of the beautiful blue valley they could never quite believe permanent. Twenty times a day, at every stream and rivulet they crossed, the older would stop and drink his fill.

"You will kill yourself with drinking, compadre," said the other, observing his companion's gasping red face and drum-tight belly.

"My son," replied he, "it is not thirst I indulge but safety. Fate has led us here, and without doubt it shall lead us back again into a desert wilderness where streams and water holes are a day apart. If here I grow lax and fail to drink my fill at every stream. thinking the next near by, I will surely perish there."

Thus they maintained caution.

Parsimony they practiced also, and tyranny over Maria. As the little herd under her care increased, her daily rations of tortillas and cheese decreased in wise proportion of her safety. A glutted child, they said, makes a careless climber.

This caution, parsimony and tyranny they regarded as custom, simplicity and benevolence, and so justified philosophy which is ever blind to the crass and superficial aspect of things seen by lesser men.

To prove it, Maria flourished. She often went out into the hills without food, and never asked for another covering when her old sheepskin wore through. The two viejos admitted satisfaction. "We are doing well by the child. She grows hardy as a weed."

Maria did not tell them that she sucked udders of milk from her herd, or that before entering the hut she hid the faded, burnt-orange blanket stolen from them. What they liked about her best was her silence.

This was the form of their lives. Its substance was

impregnated by their peculiar philosophy whose symbols gleamed palely along the top of the high stone rampart, were stacked around the outside of the hut, and held their rapt gaze inside.

The men, by night, were always squatting down before the fire with a skull between their legs. With little twigs they measured the span between its eye sockets, from gaping mouth to top of head. These lineal measurements they recorded on the dirt floor. Little triangles and squares they drew in the flickering light, and these they compared with the seasonal patterns of moon and stars on the skull of the heaven above.

Often they rose and brought out from the corner a bundle of bound twigs. Each was marked by a knife cut, a strip of peeled bark or a broken branch. These too were laid out carefully on the floor to compare with a skull.

"Yes. The wild plum branch marked with the cut of a new moon. It is the one that shows where the water rose highest in the little stream to the west."

"Pues, brother. I remember this skull well. A lively young ram—he who climbed highest always. To the gray cliffs with moss so thick in the cracks. Observe these wrinkles, compadre. What a head!"

With such remarks they punctuated hours of silent study. Maria lay on the floor, belly down, watching their intent and timeless faces. Their sharp, shrewd eyes bored through the skulls at their feet. The vast skull of the heavens they probed, and added to the zodiacal signs read in the brittle bone. Even the earth they seemed to strip of its flesh to sound the depth of springs, of winter snows and underground streams.

To them, it was all one pattern endlessly repeated in magnitude and miniature. By goat skulls they read the record of floods and droughts, foretold heavy snows and drying springs, measured the movement of stars—and little by little as men ventured up from the valley, they began to prophesy love and illfortune, wealth and sickness, danger, drying wells, and to supply remedies for heavy hearts.

To the villagers below they were charlatans and greedy thieves, or men wise and learned in the ancient learning of the hills, depending upon the opinion of those badly cheated in trade, who slyly suspected where their missing goats had gone, or happened to seduce their chiquitas soon after purchasing a love charm. To all the beautiful blue valley they were at least markedly eccentric.

But to Maria they always remained philosophers.

She was a wild and wary little goat. She saw through their charlatanry and maintained silence. Their tyranny she endured for the spot of benevolence it contained. With simple, unsuspected guile she combated their parsimony, and was not above trading a kid to a passing stranger while excusing its loss by referring to a marauding bear.

Of it all nothing endured but the intent of their teachings. The great dome of the midnight skies, and the dome of the earth rounding from horizon to horizon: both forever repeated with the triangles and squares of stars, and with the wrinkled watermarks of freshets and spring thaws, upon the lesser, miniature skulls of beast and man. This was the lesson of her childhood. She never suspected it was philosophy. She only thought that she was learning about goats.

The two viejos, then, were wise men. In their wisdom they choked out life with a high stone wall across the throat of the cañon. It had one little gate. Out of it went Maria each day with her scrawny goats, and into it was permitted to pass an occasional visitor from the valley. Inside, the two old philosophers prophesied water and weather, attended personally to their precious sheep, and confounded all men with their alarming eccentricity.

They made only one mistake—one miscalculation of water and weather. It was as though the life they shut out in front crawled around and struck them from the unsuspected rear.

It came in the form of a flood down the steep-walled,

cañon. The thunderclouds broke against the face of the cliff, were transformed into great glacial boulders as round and gray and smooth as enormous skulls. They snapped pines, tore out dirt and brush, and swept down in a raging torrent that scarce thirty minutes before had been a twinkling little trout stream.

The high stone wall, shutting out the flow of life in front, had created something of a vacuum in the pocket in back. Now the flow from behind rushed in to fill it. It was a great lesson, this trite truth that nature abhors a vacuum, but the two philosophers had no time to learn it. In a twinkling they were immersed in a torrent six feet deep. The protective goose grease of their inherent aloofness was battered by rolling stones and twisting logs. Soon their heads were too.

The little hut unfolded like a flower, the aspen fence collapsed like straw. Men, sheep and a few goats, pitiously bleating and shrieking were dashed against the stone wall. For a minute it held. Then with a crash it collapsed, and the flood swept down into the valley to leave an apron of debris, a few bloated carcasses for the buzzards, and the bodies of the two viejos whose fate had perverted their philosophy by neither drawing them back into a desert wilderness nor developing their thirst in proportion to the water they received.

Maria, up in the hills with her goats, stumbled upon a half-collapsed hut in which they took up new quarters. It stood in a little clearing just below the tall weathered cliffs that jutted out to separate the upper and lower halves of the one long valley. Often she climbed the overgrown and almost imperceptible trail to the edge of the precipice. Here, immobile as one of her goats, her long hair blowing in the wind, she stood staring fixedly down into the beautiful blue valley.

Below, the great white-cloud wagons kept passing, the fort

grew up. It was all very strange. But she was a stranger. Most people turn from the thing called life to the thing called philosophy. But Maria from philosophy was confronted by life.

3

At fifteen she was considered a little fey even by the most superstitious. This opinion was tempered by a grudging admiration for her goats. She and the flock were known throughout the valley, from mountain to plain. By day the vecinos might catch a glimpse of brown and gray trïckling like water between the pines. At night they could sometimes hear in the darkness a strange voice answering the tinkle of a bell.

"It is that queer Maria with her goats" they would say. "We shall buy cheese again tomorrow. But watch sharply! She cheated us last time. Watch but say nothing. Remember it is said she has an evil eye."

Mostly she stayed in the clearings near her little mountainside hut. But sometimes, penning her goats, she came down alone into the village. She moved as a young pine might move, neither proudly nor humbly, but self-reliant. She walked in the middle of the road as mountain folk walk in town, needing some assurance of space. And all that she saw, she devoured with the hunger of the solitary—the hunger that yet can be appeased so quickly and for so long.

Her eyes were quick and bright as a bird's. Her tongue was sharp for she used it not often enough to dull its edge. She wore a tattered dress of course, dull trade stuff. Under it her breasts hung like August plums—small and firm, not green nor yet wholly ripe. Her arms and legs were brown and bare. In the sunlight her long black hair rippled with the same queer aliveness that permeated her whole body. She was not beautiful, but she had the beauty of the wild.

Before her, fresh-plastered, new-adobe Santa Gertrudes shimmered in the hot afternoon. The walls of Bishop Lamy's new church rose clean ash-gray with adobe brought from Guadalupita. Behind it, chattering like a flock of blackbirds, the Sisters of Loretto watched their convent school being given its first coat of yellow tierra amarilla. In the row of stores, trading posts and cantinas, Maria recognized the relumbroso from the red clay banks around Turquillo. And north and south, the scattered adobes reflected white and clay-blue from Cañoncito and Chacón.

It was a single village street sprawled along the winding, rutted road between the pine hills and the cottonwoods lining the river. But with its colors the girl saw in it all the clay banks and the cañons, the hills and chalk cliffs of the one long valley she wandered from end to end.

Over all hung a haze of dust. It never settled. Great wains loaded with hay and grain for the new fort stirred it continually as they rumbled through town. Horsemen clattering in and pulling up their mounts on their hind legs in front of St. Vrain's store or old Fortier's, sprayed the loungers with powder. The twinkling centipede feet of a burro train loaded with firewood, even the plodding bare feet behind, kicked up little gritty geysers.

Men filled the long portales which jutted margins of shade into this river of dust. A few tobacco-spitting trappers in buckskin who lingered yet in the twilight of their time, a row of squatting Indians hunting lice—all hugging in their silence the silence of the hills. Wagon-masters and mule-skinners too, bragging on their exaggerated eight miles a day across the Jornada; a gambler with polished boots and the shirt studs of Sutter's gold; a sharp-nosed Armijo who ever deigned in his haughtiness to see the gringos at its end. Paisanos and gente de razón, strangers and homefolk, they spit and swore, laughed, drank, gambled and swapped knives, talked or discoursed in pregnant silence, and were jostled by the stream of villagers plodding past. A lady between high French heels and a Spanish comb stepped daintily over a pile of manure in the street. Father Abel lifted his hat in passing and garbled a Spanish phrase. There was a sudden roar and clatter; the whole street hushed. It was old Fortier, the trader, stamping his feet and howling in French—he had run out of sugar again. The street resumed its talk.

It was the beautiful blue valley's three races fusing in their short and transient hour. Their color and life, their customs and tongues, the strange and the familiar, the goat girl saw as she passed slowly down the street. But it was the gray, gritty dust that bit into her senses. The vast cloud that covered and muted everything, the dust to which all would finally return.

It was, in a way, the philosophy through which Maria always stared as if through a curtain.

But even it seemed to lift and dissipate when lights leapt out to sting the hide of approaching darkness. There were campfires beside the wagons and along the stream, ocote torches stuck in wall crevices of the little mud huts. Candles guttered on crowded bars and inside the church. In the stores brass lamps lit up shelves, boxes, bales. . . . Thus successively they lighted Maria's way back up the road.

She had done her little trading: goat cheese and two pelts for a bit of salt, a piece of cloth and four iron nails. Alone she had eaten beside her own fire at the edge of town. And now refreshed by food, by light and smell, she was arrested by a strange and wonderful sound.

Ójala! What a beautiful, wondrous sound! It was at once

rippling over rocks, a child's laugh, the tinkle of frosty stars. It was the blood of springtime beating an arpeggio at temples and fingertips.

But it seemed to come from the corner parlor of the huge, sprawling inn fronting the plaza. A crowd of loiterers on the portal was staring through the cracked shutters of the front windows. Maria crept round the corner, along the dark road toward the river.

The garden gate was open. Inside she could glimpse the small placita, and beyond, the enclosed garden. A light bathed the flagstones with milk, and shimmered like moonlight through the branches of a great locust. Around the tree were tethered some horses. By the saddles she knew they belonged to soldiers from the fortaleza.

Between them she crept closer to the window. A hand on their flanks, a muzzle fondled, a whisper in their ears—they were still.

Maria crept closer against the adobe wall. By standing on her toes she could see the light. It hung from the ceiling by three golden chains, a great glowing drop of goat's milk painted with red flowers. But it revealed nothing of the wonderful sound, the tinkle of the unseen frosty stars. Maria laid down her bundle, crossed hands over her breast. The smoke rising from the porcelain lamp was the incense of her tribute.

When the unseen music ended, Maria opened her eyes.

Underneath the lamp a table stood in the middle of the room. On it lay a big conch shell and a brass bound Bible. Around the walls hung a few tin daguerrotypes. Under them, on stiff red plush chairs, sat the gringo soldiers more stiffly upright in their uniforms. All faced, in the far corner, a large box of shiny redwood. Out of it protruded a brass crank.

This polished box was muy importante. Maria had seen it the day it came—from across the plains, and even across the sea, the men said. It was raining, and the wagon had bogged down in mud. Four mules couldn't drag it out. The gringo colonel had sloshed around cursing, his men had thrown over the box their own coats, and stood there heaving like whipped dogs.

So Maria waited outside, her curiosity fixed on the box, her longing on the wonderful sound now stilled.

Beside the box sat the gringo colonel's lady. Her dress foamed out from her narrow waist like a waterfall, but her face was carved from a cold white icicle. She had a narrow, cruel mouth and shallow eyes which froze when she spoke to those of the soldiers without much braid on their uniforms. She sat with her gloved hands in her lap. The soldiers sat with hands in laps.

They were gente de razón, and so they talked as people of reason always talk. The movement of their lips was ceaseless as running water, and the murmur of their strange hard voices aroused in the girl a subdued apprehension. Talk without gesture, without smiles, frowns or animation—the gringo talk which holds all and gives nothing.

So held by a mystery greater than silence itself, Maria stood peering into the room as into a lake in moonlight.

Then into the passionless stability of the parlor strode the step of life. It bore a tall, square-shouldered cavalryman. His blue eyes smiled, his curving silent mouth spoke louder than their greetings. He was a Samson whose tawny strength flowed from him in long waves that hung to his collar.

He was young but a man. The soldados, even they with beards and much gold braid, answered his manhood with quick bows. But it was the woman who answered his youth. The icicle of her face flushed, she rose and gave him her two gloved hands.

Maria saw behind the colonel's bearded smile, and smiled to herself in the darkness. "There will be a fight," she thought. "Perhaps with knives. Or maybe with the short guns. It is good!" And her strength flowed forth to that of the young man, he like a lion with the tawny mane.

But instead, a Mexican criada shuffled into the room on

bare feet carrying glasses and a bottle. They drank cautiously as men afraid of their wine, and from glasses no bigger than a goat's teats.

Suddenly the young soldado jumped up, laughed and went to the big polished box. He twirled round the brass handle, opened the lid and put in his hand.

With the first sound from the music box, Maria shrank against the wall. Una caja de música! she thought ecstatically. Magic box!

It spoke. It sang! With the voice of rippling water and of wind, it sang, with a child's laugh and the tinkle of frosty stars. And all these voices were one voice, and it was the young soldado, its master.

He stood there, one hand on the box, staring directly into her eyes with cloudy eyes and a quiet smile. Maria shook in the darkness. Her blood became water, wine, fire; her thoughts nebulous as clouds drifting across the face of a moon. She shrank back into the darkness, but not away. Her face grew hot. She held her breasts as if they were the warm, struggling body of a new-born kid in her arms.

Then suddenly the music stopped; he turned around, laughing, to his companions.

Maria ducked, grabbed up her bundle and fled. She had not yet learned that there are things one cannot escape.

For two months Maria kept out of Santa Gertrudes. She did her little trading in San Antonio, and led her goats into the northern cañons. The short grass of an August drought was the excuse that brought her back across La Cañada and the Coyote.

She sat on the slopes overlooking the beautiful blue valley now sere and brown in summer sunshine. Her goats scrambled at will up the rocky hillside, straying through scrub oak and dribbling between the metallic, dusty pines above. Always the faint tinkle of a bell marked their casual whereabouts. Maria seldom turned around.

What held her gaze was the continual stream of dust that rolled, wave after wave, up the cañon to the fort sixteen kilómetros away. In these waves, as they passed below, she detected loaded wagons or burro trains, valley horsemen, or occasionally the uniform of a galloping soldier. Maria shrugged. These gringo soldados! In hats they all looked alike.

Late in the afternoon she rose and led her goats down to water. The little stream crawled half-alive through thickets of chokecherry and wild plum. Here she splashed in a tiny pool, and rubbed her body with grass. Slowly she pulled on her single coarse dress and stretched out like a lizard in the sun to dry her hair.

That afternoon Maria was asleep when one of the waves of dust, like a worn out ripple, subsided in the road a half mile away. Out of it a lone horseman turned off into the brush. His polished boots were covered with dust, his tunic unbuttoned, his face red and sweaty. At the glade he dismounted, throwing the reins over the head of his horse which stood unmoving while he walked down to the water.

He was master of the song which had caught up with Maria, but mastered for a moment by silence. A big bluebottle fly buzzed among the plums. A single pine murmured in the breeze. Far off came the faint tinkle of a bell, and nearby the patter of another goat. Maria still slept.

Before her the gringo soldier lay at the edge of the stream as some men lay at the edge of a precipice: belly down, arms outstretched, head cautiously forward. Drinking his fill, he raised up to a squat and splashed his arms and face.

"Major! Here boy!"

As the horse trotted obediently forward to take his turn, Maria roused. She awoke instantly alive and with the intense awareness of an animal—head up, a hand on the huaraches under her head, one bare brown leg outstretched for instant flight.

What she saw before her was a wet tangle of tawny hair,

staring blue eyes, a familiar red face and the uniform of a gringo soldado. He too was caught in a posture of surprise, in the act of wiping off his mouth with the back of his hand as he turned around. It was as if he had stifled a song on his lips—this tawny-haired master of the singing box whose heart had once spoken to her in the darkness.

"Cómo le va! Cómo . . . . "

His Spanish was terrible, his breath faintly warmed with the smell of the drink which had flushed his face. But in his eyes was mirrored something of her long, bare brown legs, the dark fell of her freshly washed hair, and the quick, dark look in her own eyes—the unsung song which answered his own.

Major stopped, his black velvet ears flung forward: it was pitched too high for even them. He tramped heavily down to the stream. Drinking, he raised his head and regarded the two on the bank. Then, as if seeing no more than he heard, he turned his back and began to munch grass.

His master had taken off his tunic to sit on. "No habla Inglés?" he stuttered. "Caliente, eh? . . . Jesus, it's hot! I've got a long ride back."

"Sí" A flat, uncommunicative sí. The goat girl's tattered dress was still up around her bare smooth thighs, but she had brushed her tangle of hair. She wiggled her toes, and chewed a blade of grass. Her casual manner marked an inward trepidation. She felt a weakness and a strength stealing upon her, both at once and the same, a strange thing.

"Fumar . . . cigarro?" the man mumbled, sitting up to fumble through his pockets.

Without waiting, Maria reached behind for her bundle, and took out a little sack of punche and a roll of corn husks. She rolled herself a cigarette and smoked. Now, propped up on one elbow, she could see him more closely: the fine gold hairs on the backs of his hands; the straight line dividing his sunburned face from his white chest—like a cut throat; and the dancing stars in his eyes.

"Me . . . yo montar a caballo. . . . To the fort. Over there."
He pointed over the hills. "Soldier, sabe? I go pretty quick."

But he didn't. He only rubbed his brass buttons, dusted off
his boots, whistled a bar of "Yankee Doodle," grinned.

Maria's face remained calm, inscrutable, almost somber—
the look of a child which is interested in everything, knowing
nothing, and hence incapable of surprise. It is the same look
of old women of the world who have seen through it and
expect nothing. But the smile had quickened her blood to the
beat of a song that seemed oddly old and familiar though she
could not remember its tune. And he kept smiling—closer
now.

He suddenly pinched her bare toes. Maria yanked up her
legs, broke out into a giggle. To recover from this astounding
relapse into the unfamiliar world of childhood, she raised up
and whistled shrilly through her teeth. Far off in the brush
answered the tinkle of a bell. Reassured, like a general, of the
legion at her command, she was again calm and enigmatic.
But the young adjutant had not released her toes. His hand
slid casually up to her knee and settled there lightly as a bird
on a branch. This time Maria did not giggle, nor did she
whistle to her goats.

"I got to get back. To the fort. Over there, sobre las
montañas," he said after a time in an empty voice, as if to
himself.

"Cómo no?"

Why not, indeed? For it was a strange thing that as this
weakness grew upon her, so did the strength it held.

So through the afternoon neither moved. The goats stirred
like phantoms through the brush. Major crunched grass with
the bit still between his teeth. A magpie chattered in the
pine, a hawk hung suspended overhead. The stream rippled
noisily in the silence. It was all one song, a song heard by
none but sung by all. And in the yellowing sunlight the wild
August plums hung darker, softer—green no longer, but yet
not wholly ripe.

Man and woman sprawled closer together now in a sleep that was not a sleep nor yet wakefulness. It was the still trance of August and twilight, between day and night, when all things have grown and wait in tranquillity for harvest and fulfillment.

They sat up suddenly, as if conscious of the shouts of mule skinners passing on the road as they had all afternoon.

"I ought to be goin' back to the fort," the soldier said, staring at a tuft of dust shot through by the fire of the setting sun. But instead he tethered Major out of sight in the brush. Maria called softly to her goats, as if merely to hear their crackling in the thicket.

The shadow of the pine grew longer, blacker. A breeze was coming up. And yet neither man nor woman spoke.

When the sun went down they moved back into the wild plum thicket. Here it was warmer, darker, and there was nothing to be seen or heard, not even the faint ecstatic trembling of the plums overhead. . . .

The moon was lifting when they came out. The cliffs were gray and ghostly across the stream. In the open glade the ewes stirred uneasily, full of milk. Major whinnied. It was a strange place. It had changed tone. The man and the woman looked around them as if they had emerged to unfamiliar surroundings.

The soldier came back to reality quicker. "Dammit to hell!" he growled, loosening his horse. "The colonel ordered me back at dark!"

Maria understood his tone but not the words. She stood caressing his hat, and did not answer. He grabbed it from her, slapped it on his head. Now he swiftly buttoned up his tunic. What a strange man, once his tawny hair was hid. In hats and brass buttons all gringo soldados looked alike.

He was on his horse now, and Maria, barefooted, was standing quietly, arms down at her sides.

"Here!" He suddenly leaned down and thrust some trinkets into her hand. "Adiós, muchacha! Don't let the goats run off with you!"

Maria watched Major lope across the moonlit glade, his great strides springy as a cat's on the grassy turf. And far up the road, in darkness, she could hear his receding gallop.

When he was gone, she examined the thin little gold piece in her hand. On one side was engraven a star and through a tiny hole ran a piece of blue ribbon. This was very nice. And he had left her also one of his brass buttons.

She tucked them away in her bundle, and then went out to count her goats.

At the foot of the pine Maria buried her brass button and the gold piece with its blue ribbon. It was a shallow little hole between two roots, and covered with a flat rock—very easily dug out every week or two when she returned with her goats.

On one of her visits something strange happened. The thin gold piece broke open in her hands. In one inside half was a little picture. It was the face of a gringo lady. Maria gave a little scream of delight. "Bonita! Qué bonita!" She looked closer, and then murmured awesomely, "Verdad, verdad!" Without doubt it was the face of the colonel's lady. This was a wonderful thing, and Maria was more pleased than ever.

She stayed there all day, the brass button in her lap and the gold piece hung round her throat on its ribbon so that she could look at it from time to time. Lackadaisically she watched the road, but was never disappointed when their giver did not return. Like all gringo soldados, he was a little unreal, evanescent as his song. The trinkets he had left became themselves unreal, and had no value in nor connection with her daily life. As fetishes they were simply symbols of an August eve, and so she left them each time in the only spot where they had validity.

The twilights came quicker, they faded from gold to brass, took on the greenish hue of leaf mold with the first frost. The picture streaked and faded, the blue ribbon rotted, the brass tarnished, the gold became encrusted with loam. With the passing of summer they too lost their power. Maria left them buried there, and no longer returned. By winter she had almost forgotten them.

One day in early April, Maria came down from her hut into San Antonio. As she left the trading post, an old woman hobbled out into the muddy road after her. She was lean and wrinkled, with one sharp eye, and for fingers the prehensile talons of a hawk—the village midwife. The eye played over Maria's broadened hips, the two wild plums of her breasts now full and ripe, her cold pinched face. One long curved talon prodded the girl in the side. Then she thumped Maria's belly.

"You—daughter of many goats—things are going well?"

"Cómo no, Madre?" Maria answered easily.

"You are plumper than a full moon. You are shorter winded than a blown cow. Mark my words, you will not climb after your goats long."

"Verdad, Madre. But the trail down was steep and the drifts deep. I shall work off my weakness with spring; have I not always followed my goats?"

"Pues!" snorted the old woman. "You are with child. It will be but another moon."

Maria lifted her foot out of one puddle into another, and swung her gaze along the snowy ridgetop. "Sí. It is what I have often thought, of late, that I shall have a child. Pues! Have I not seen my ewes bear each spring?"

"Mother of God! Are you girl or goat?" For a moment she regarded the girl with the shrewd appraisal of her one eye. "It was a soldier then? Another gringo soldado from the fortaleza? Todos Santos! He knows already, doubtless. Or shall I be the one to tell him, who have caught so many others loose-tongued over their bottles?"

To this prodding Maria gave a puzzled frown. "A soldier? Oh yes. Doubtless, Madre. But how should he know, and why? I have never seen him since."

"Ah, a soldier then! As I knew." The old partera threw

back her dirty rebozo and rubbed her hands together. "Now tell me. Did he have many brass buttons or few? Was he one who spoke or one who listened to a master? Was he of those who are black, or one of the six with flaming hair? He whispered his name in your ear, perchance? You know the sound of his horse's feet in the dark? Speak quickly!"

"Mi Madre," answered Maria quietly, "you talk only in words. In hats and brass buttons all soldiers look alike."

The old woman vainly braced herself against this assault of ignorance or loyalty. In either case she saw her expectations of bribery and a fat fee dissipate like smoke.

"Fool! Fool! Burro! Fool! It is what one can expect from a girl in the hills, wilder than her goats—and one who is blinded by the song of a crow! But stay, child, listen!" She caught Maria by the shoulder. Her cracked, greedy voice lowered to a confidential whine. "It is the way of the world, of women and soldiers. You have known another? We shall tell him, eh? Trust it to me, niña! There are men in this world who are fathers but for my words. Who knows the difference save God, the priest, and a few chosen few?"

"I do not understand," said Maria. "It is cold. My bundle is heavy, my legs tired already. I go. Adiós, Madre."

"Go? When then shall we talk business? Come, niña. We shall agree on the price. You neither know the soldier or another who would do as well. You are entirely without man. You are poor. Your time comes quickly. Shall we say a goat? Perhaps that old ewe I have seen straggling behind?"

"Por Dios! For what? That you should have my best ewe?"

"Santa Maria! Are you a goat to crawl in a thicket when your time comes? Who shall watch the phases of your moon, petition the saints, gather herbs, make tea, measure your belly, count the heartbeats of him inside? Who shall alleviate your pain with wisdom, stroke your forehead, mark the cross on your breasts and seize upon the instant as a swooping hawk to pluck forth the first fruit of your womb with untellable ease? Who but I, who follows men's passions and women's frailties from mountain to plain, who has delivered nigh half the souls of this valley to the sun of day—the best partera from Las Colonias to the Cebollita. And the cheapest, niña! Come! Shall we say a fat ewe? With perhaps a bit of cheese each week until the happy throes of pain clutch at your belly, and you cry wildly for these practiced old hands, this stout heart and all the knowledge of the new ways?"

"I had not thought it so important—this simple thing of having a child," murmured Maria vaguely. "But perhaps, as you say, a bit of advice . . . a simpática. . . ."

"Bueno! A ewe then! And the cheese? A bit now on this cold winter day?"

"Pues, but Madre. A child—truly that is something. I have never had a child before. But a goat. Yes. A goat is something else. They are my friends, my compadres, my children too. And the cheese. Mother!" she said resolutely, "we shall say perhaps a goat. But certainly not my best ewe, who lags behind because her bag is heavy. But a goat. Yes, perhaps a goat."

So a month and a shaving later, Maria parted with one of her herd. It seemed a needless extravagance, and never again did she succumb to the luxury of a partera. What she really bought was a vast knowledge of midwifery, and the sound of another human voice and the touch of a hand in the loneliness of her little mountainside hut.

The child, she reflected, would have come anyway. It was a boy. The old woman called it Teodosio—her favorite name. So did Maria later.

His coming made little difference in her life. He simply added to the weight of the bundle she carried about, leading her goats. In truth, Teodosio was never much. He was rachitic and sickly, and his apathy grew into the incurable disease of laziness. Maria always called him the runt of a litter. Her phrase contained the germ of endearment. It did not come until she really began to notice him. He had black hair, dark eyes and iodine-colored skin. This lent her some satisfaction, for by then there was throughtout the valley a scatter of queer-looking children, dark skinned youngsters with red hair, and some with thick lips, wide fleshy nostrils and negroid cheeks.

It was not Teodosio then, but the first ripe August after his coming that reminded Maria of the gringo soldado and the trinkets buried at the foot of the pine. She carried the boy there. Squirrels or water had scooped out her hiding place between the roots. Without its fetishes, the place had lost its validity. It seemed just one glade of many.

Maria settled down, her back to the road, and suckled the child on her lap. There had been rain in the mountains, the stream ran full and noisily. In the glade the grass was high. The thickets were heavy with plums. In the hot stillness of the afternoon her goats wandered sleepily after the tinkle of a bell. Maria was well content.

4

Maria at eighteen had given up rambling the cañons with her goats. She had moved down from her mountainside hut to live with a young muleteer at the bottom of the cliffs. They had a new girl child whose smiling aliveness balanced Teodosio's sullen laziness. In front of their squat, two-room adobe, their few varas of land sloped down into the valley. Behind was a rocky corral to hold the last of Maria's goats, a pig, four mules and a great wagon.

The piece of hillside with its adobe lent them stability, the mules and wagon a meager living, and the children sanctified their love.

A little of the wildness went out of Maria's eyes. Her body, grown heavier, no longer moved with the alert stealthiness of an animal. Her voice lost its faintly hollow sound as her ears grew accustomed to hearing it answered by something besides an echo. She did not become soft. She was up an hour before dawn to beat Onesimo's tortillas thin, and her furious calp-clap-clap resounded again at dark like an assault against time and loneliness.

Onesimo was a man of twenty-two. His long thin body covered with hand-dressed leather looked like a monk's in brown sackcloth. He had a lean ascetic face sallow in tone. It sloped backward from a weak chin jutting a few uncut hairs to a narrow smooth forehead, and the slant was continued by his straight black hair combed back over his small round head. He thus appeared to be continually gazing upward—like a martyr tied to a cross and searching the heavens for an echo of his faith. He was a simple, credulous fellow, he had long and kind though calloused hands, and was an excellent mule skinner.

Onesimo hauled grain, hay and wood to the fort, leaving Maria with her girl child, her work and goats. Often he took Teodosio.

"Who knows?" Maria would say. "Perhaps there will come the day when you recognize his father, he with tawny hair. You have asked among the others, Onesimo? Qué lástima! No doubt he grieves, believing his loins dry and seedless."

"I ask, but am answered with laughter. It is as if God permits his ignorance. . . . But still, as I have said, there was talk among the soldiers of him whom the colonel sent angrily away because of this lady. But I shall ask." And Onesimo mildly drove away with Teodosio beside him.

Maria shrugged and went out to the wood pile with her axe. It was difficult to remind herself from time to time of the almost forgotten gringo soldado. In her happiness she somehow felt that she had done him ill. But at the fort soldiers came and soldiers went. And soon no more new soldiers came, and troop by troop all the old ones left—even the red-faced colonel. Onesimo told her that the fortaleza was empty as a last year's magpie nest. Only the dust marched down the parade ground, the wind and the rain ate at the walls. She herself felt Santa Gertrudes go dead and barren. And in the great inn the French music box with its quadrilles, polkas and valses alone remained to gather cobwebs in the unused parlor.

Onesimo lost his big wagon and three of his mules. With the fourth he plowed his bit of rocky ground. Maria followed behind. With a sharp stick she poked holes in the earth, and dropped into each a kernel of corn. All over the valley people were doing the same. The gold and silver, the laughter and riot, the soldiers and all the gringos had gone. But the land remained, and the people dug in to sink their roots.

Maria and Onesimo were still ambitious. They wanted to get married and have the children baptized, all at once—perhaps on Christmas. This, thought Onesimo, would be very nice.

"On the very nacimiento of Nuestro Señor," he would say at night. "On the day that the Christ child lay in the little barn with the cows and horses and chickens and pigs about him. Humble like ourselves, Maria." And he would reach down his long, kind and calloused hand to a goat or a pig huddling up to him for warmth. "He, Our Lord, will bless our love. We shall be man and wife on paper like any gente de razón, and be much respected. And the children. Ójala! The holy water will dedicate them to God. Niña, what shall we name the niña, the first of my seed? It must be just so. Inocencia? Is not her smile chaste? Quiteria? Purísima Concepción?—though to be sure it was but the desire for your ripe breasts and eager body that drove me up the cliffs those many nights before you came to me here. Serafin? Ah, but wait till you see the angels painted in the church, like God's doves, with silver wings. Macedonia? Fidencia Eutima? Pues—it will come, the proper name for our niña. The priest will reveal God's will."

Maria had little to say. She had never been to church. But from Onesimo she was learning much of God, of Jesú Cristo and all the Saints. She could not be fanatically devout as Onesimo who wore a cross under his shirt, carved another for the house, spoke of the Saints more familiarly than of his friends, and to whom the Passion was the greatest thing he could conceive. Maria lacked the imagination which makes saints of fools, martyrs of fanatics, and lends grace and strength to the most humble of men.

In all the stories she saw only the human frailty and the human triumph of their holy participants. Joseph in the pit; Peter at his nets; Daniel walking unarmed among lions— "Verdad? And no staff, not even a knife? Santísima! I cannot imagine such mountain lions!" Judas she forgave. "For why did not El Señor give him the thirteen pieces of gold first? He who could make a thousand fishes from one surely would not begrudge a poor man a few pesos for his tortillas. Could He not take care of Himself as well?" But Jesús she liked. She imagined him riding down the dusty valley road astraddle a burro, "the short and simple animal of the poor." A long lean man, with narrow kind hands and thin ascetic face, His long legs dangling to the ground. He reminded her of Onesimo. And when He found He had no power really, and the soldados drove great iron nails through His narrow kind hands and limp dusty feet, and He leaned His head back upon the cross to stare upward into the heavens for an echo of His faith—ah, then Maria's heart cried out with comprehension. "Pobrecito! Pobrecito Jesús! And no doubt the crows and buzzards swooped down to eat out His eyes. How much better had this poor Jesús gone into the hills with some goats, had He trusted to the earth and not the heavens!"

They were great men, these Saints, the Father's Son and His Holy Twelve. But deep in her heart their religion seemed less than that of those two old philosophers who had taught her that even the skulls of goats reflect the pattern of the stars and the power of the earth below. So secretly she climbed the cliffs to the little hut wherein she had lived alone, there to consult signs of the future.

They told no more than Onesimo's little wooden box with its diminishing silver pesos which he had been saving for the ceremony. "There are but half enough," he would say. "No longer they grow, but dwindle. Yet the priests are kind. They will take the money and a promise to God for the rest. Have no fear."

On Christmas Eve they set out for midnight mass. Maria on the mule, wrapped in rebozo and blanket, and carrying the niña. Teodosio behind on the rump. And Onesimo walking ahead to lead the beast. Like Joseph, thought Maria, leading another Mary to another village on a cold December night. And she watched his tall lean figure plodding in front, head up as if he were guided by a bright, mounting star, his left hand stuck inside his leather coat to feel the little buckskin sack of pesos against his breast.

The night was clear and cold, the valley a long crescent lake of blue between the steep black hills. There were patches of snow on the lower pine slopes. The peaks cut sharp and white into the sky. But because the roads were hard and dry, the valley was alive with travelers. They were coming down the cañons from Chacón and Guadalupita, up from La Cueva, across the campo from Los Altos and over the hills from Ledoux. Lone horsemen. Groups of six or seven on patient, pattering burros. Families en todo huddled between straw and blankets in creaking wagons.

"Adiós!" they called in passing, their muffled voices rising into the dark, cold stillness.

"Adiós!" answered Onesimo in his low proud voice.

Adiós! Adiós! The synonymous word of greeting and farewell of a people who know their transiency upon the wide and bitter earth.

It was nearly midnight when they plodded into Santa Gertrudes. Two bonfires lit up the crowded plaza; on top the walls luminarias were burning, little rows of flickering flames. It all had a queer, still aliveness, a vatic hush. Even the chiming of the frosty bells. So that the people walked quickly, stealthily and without greeting from their tethered mounts and wagons.

The posadas were over. But in Pierre Fortier's window, lit by two candles, gleamed the manger of Bethlehem. The box was filled with straw. In it lay the Holy Family, tiny wooden figures, and horses, cows, goats, a rooster of red cedar. Overhead hung a tin star.

"Bonita! Qué bonita!" Maria clapped her numb hands. But Onesimo knelt stiffly in the road and raked off his hat in silence.

Now, swung with the stream, they stepped humbly into the church. Maria gasped. With her first look, religion took on for her the awesome splendor of gold and gilt and brass, of silk and lace, of shinning light. She forgot the long lean man with a thin gentle face, the humble Jesus riding down the dusty road on a burro. She forgot how His narrow kind hands and limp dusty feet had been peirced with great iron nails, the meekness and humbleness of His teachings. She forgot, as all men since have forgotten, the creed of the spirit. And she saw only what all men see—the ornate, splendid and confusing temple of its impressive and meaningless outward form.

Maria was not aware that in one instant something within her had refuted forever Onesimo's faith. She was too dumbfounded at that cavernous temple of unbelievable splendor with its huge carven vigas, each in its time a lofty pine and now bedecked again with fresh branches, with its hundred santos and tapestries, its thousand candles gleaming everywhere, its altar magnificent beyond her imagination. Madre! Was it possible? Here? In Santa Gertrudes?

Onesimo was abashed too, and Maria could not understand his hesitation. Was he not devout, no stranger to this church of God? They were still standing just inside the doors. Onesimo, hat off and carrying Teodosio, and Maria with her rebozo covering both the niña and her own face so that only her eyes peeked out.

The church was packed; a few rows of benches in front, then more villagers sitting stolidly on chairs they had carried from home, and in back and down the aisles more and more people crowding in to kneel on the hard, uneven planks.

Pushed from behind, Maria started forward. But Onesimo

gently plucked her shawl, and humbly led her to the cold back corner. "We shall kneel here with the poor and the sinful," he whispered. "I have not paid for these many months. Besides, it is only the gente de razón who have seats in front."

Above them a candle in an iron socket dripped tallow down the wall. By its guttering light Maria could see Onesimo's face. It held a strange soft look of adoration and abnegation. He head was tilted backward, so that his long uncut hair hung down on his greasy leather coat. His eyes were closed. He was mumbling inaudibly through trembling lips.

So in cold and candlelight, in wonder and adoration, they knelt praying God to forgive them their ununderstood sins and the weak flesh that cramped and cringed from the hard, cold floor. A column of children filed past carrying pine branches and candles. An unseen chorus wailed "Ave Maria." A priest paraded, head down and swinging a little pot that perfumed the air. And all this sound and smell and movement beat vainly, like waves, against the jutting altar.

An incomprehensible ritual held them at bay. Candles were lit and snuffed, books opened and snapped shut, altar cloths laid and folded up. Two priests controlled the magic. A young slim one who had paraded with the fragrant pot, and an old fat one. When they knelt, stiffly as if in a great hurry, Maria could see the young one's close-cropped bullet head. When they turned around she watched the old one's white fat hands fluttering at his chest like birds, also in a hurry. They rang little bells, lifted crosses and forever kept up a low mumble in a strange tongue. This impressed Maria. She knew it was the language of God which only they could understand.

But now the old fat one spoke the Spanish, and then the gringo. His Spanish was queerly slurred. He spoke it as one of the arrogant viejos contemptuously referred to by the people of the valley as "Don Thinco Thentavos de Athucar." But

Maria listened patiently. He was talking of José y Maria, the gentle Jesús and how all men should be simpático, simple and poor.

The mass ended. People pushed forward for a sip of Christ's blood and a taste of the bread which was His flesh. Many, like Onesimo, crawled all the way down front on their knees. Maria waited in the corner. She suckled the niña again, then roused Teodosio from the sheepskin on the floor.

The doors were opened. Christmas Day stood on the threshold, cloaked in darkness and bitter cold. The people with eyes still lit by wonder trudged out to their horses and wagons. Only Onesimo and Maria remained, each with a child in his arms.

"Come, Maria," he said smiling gently. "It is the moment. The Christ is born. We shall be united in His name."

They walked slowly down the empty church, and halted at the railing before the altar. The young slim priest was hurriedly snuffing candles. He had taken off his robe, undone his collar.

Onesimo laid down Teodosio, still sleepily whining, and threw over the boy his sheepskin. "Padre, mi padre!" he called softly. "Un momentito, one word in the name of God." Hat in hand he walked toward the priest in the flickering candlelight. Maria waited patiently in the gelid gloom. The silence was sepulchral. It was broken by Onesimo's low impassioned voice and the sharp queries of the priest.

"Si, Padre, si, si! We would wait no longer. Our bodies have been joined by the the fire of passion. Let now our union be tempered with the Holy Water and the cooling faith of Him born this night. Mira! Our niña waits for a name."

"But now? Near dawn? What is this? Does not the good padre give days for marrying and send word from village to village? My eyes see yet another child. He is well grown. You and this woman have waited long. How now would you hurry? The mass has tired the padre. I myself am sleepy.

Come again, my son."

"But I have money. Look. In this little bag."

The priest hefted the buckskin bag in his hand. "There is very little, more will be needed," he answered reluctantly. "But I shall call the padre. Padre! Blessed Father!"

From a room behind the altar the old, fat padre came out. His eyes were small and cunning, his jaw resolute, his hands fat and white. Maria, from the darkness, saw that he had laid away the grace of God with his robe. He scratched himself like a man.

Onesimo did not see the scratching. He had knelt at the padre's feet for a blessing. The fat white hands were over his head, but they were counting the pesos poured from the little buckskin bag.

"It is a strange request," the young priest was saying. "There is the matter of writing the papers, for one thing. There is tomorrow and the day after, there are the regular days for marrying. Perhaps the Lord will not permit His gracious servant to be so unduly tired at such a time of night. All this have I pointed out. Yet there is this to be said, God always welcomes new lambs into the fold. See, there are two. Look also, the man is humble but devout, though stubborn. And he has brought money. Did you count it, Padre? Pues! You have promised the rest soon, my son?"

"Sí, seguro! Certainly, mis padres. To God I promised the rest. Are we not humble but honest?" Onesimo stood up then with a face illumined by anticipation.

The padre scowled. He had pocketed the pesos: they would, no doubt, stop his scratching. As he carelessly handed back to Onesimo the limp buckskin bag, his fat white hand lifted. He grasped Onesimo's long lean face by the chin and turned it into the full glare of a candle.

"God permits my memory to fail, but my eyes never. I have seen you before." His small eyes glittered coldly. "Yes, I saw you often. Then suddenly you came no more."

Onesimo's face, released, dropped into the shadow. His

long thin body went boneless. "I had no money," he said tonelessly. "When the gringo soldados left the fortaleza I had no work. Three mouths there were to feed. But God I did not forget. Padre, I remembered! I am here now." His voice strengthened. Maria saw him raise his face.

But in the padre's she saw a sullen anger. It flamed up in his eyes, his voice.

"Do you lie? Here before God?" he thundered. "Confess where you have been, and others! That certain group of men who think to take the worship of God into their own hands. Los Hermanos they call themselves. Brothers of Sangre de Cristo. Brothers! Brothers of iniquity! Brothers of sin and evil practices! Have I not denounced such practices, according to the blessed instructions of the Archbishop Salpointe from God?" His voice beat at Onesimo, at the young priest, at Maria waiting in the darkness. "That is where you have been, evil man, Brother of Evil! On your knees, sinner! Confess that from such cursed practices you have crept into this Holy House!"

But strangely, it seemed to Maria, Onesimo did not fall to his knees. Boneless and contrite, yet curiously resolute, his long thin body stood before the priest.

"Pecado, pecado," he said in a hushed, low voice. "I have sinned, but my sins will be forgiven for I have remembered God. And so I have come with my woman to be united in His name."

The padre's fat white face had gone red. The little blue veins stuck out. He shook his fist at the high honey-colored vigas. "You do not confess! You do not name your evil Brothers! Mother of God! But I shall learn. Dios tarda pero no olvida. Yes! God delays but does not forget. In His name these cursed Brothers, these evil flagellants will be excluded from the Church. Hah!" He seized Onesimo by his leather coat, stood peering into the lean ascetic face. "And then what? They will be excommunicated!"

Maria heard the young priest gasp beside him. But from

57

Onesimo she heard nothing. Only his face seemed to have grown more sallow as he stared upward over the padre's head.

The priest misjudged his silence. "It is a warning to you who would escape God's eyes and come here for His blessing. And now," he added curtly, "go and reflect upon your sin. Until you return to confess there will be no talk of marrying. And see that you tell others—that I, their good father, have the eyes of Heaven."

And so in cold and darkness they plodded home under the frosty stars. Maria on the mule, wrapped in rebozo and blanket, and carrying the niña still nameless. Teodosio on the rump. And Onesimo's tall lean body plodding in front, head up as if he were guided by a fading star, his left hand stuck inside his leather coat to feel the empty buckskin bag against his breast.

Maria was a little confused.

"I do not think we shall be married," she said when the plodding mule stopped before their hut.

Onesimo gently lifted down Teodosio, then took the niña in his arms. "No, I do not think we shall be married," he assented in his low proud voice.

Maria sighed without understanding or regret. The pallid wintry dawn was seeping over the valley walls. The earth, timeless and immense, had not changed. It was all as before.

In spring too the valley is beautiful and blue, but the beauty is muted and the blue diminished by the intense white light of the steadily rising sun. The mountain walls shrink back. The valley lifts. It is only one ampitheater of many in a vast continental plateau. And so it reflects the mystic strangeness and inimical austerity of the greater whole.

Occasional clouds of apricot, peach and wild plum blossom soften the harshness in the river bottoms below. They repeat the variolitic white splotches of snow and ice and sleet in the cañons above. Both are ephemeral white shadows on the face of the dark enduring earth. Its features are the red sandstone cliffs, the sandy hillocks of yucca, the bare red-brown earth and the chocolate mud banks along the lower river. Its expression is fixed and inimical, and the same look of strained attention and repellent remoteness is seen in the faces of the people. It is as if the brilliant blinding light reveals their common soul.

Maria could see it in Onesimo's vacuous, bloodshot eyes as she saw it at twilight when the Sangre de Cristo took on the color of their name. Thus she first understood the Brothers of Light, the Brothers of the Blood of Christ, divining dimly the ununderstood truth that faiths like everything else spring from and are distorted by their earth.

Onesimo was still kind and humble, simpático always. He never referred to his disappointing visit to the priest, to their conversation, nor did he ever return to church. Yet little by little he changed. He neglected his rockly fields to wander up the cañons. When he returned at night he would sit brooding in the corner. His eyes became vibrating pools of light. His tall lean body grew leaner, his long ascetic face thinner. Suddenly he lay with her no more, and slept beside Teodosio on a sheepskin.

This religion business! Maria fought faith with faith. She clapped out his tortillas ever thinner, hoed the weeds, held her tongue, and was more than mindful of Teodosio and Niña.

"You are a good and a discreet woman," said Onesimo gently. "But there are things women do not understand."

Gradually she learned a bit here and there from other women working in the fields. They too were not slept with, held their tongues and maintained caution lest the padre at church learn too much. Their men too were Hermanos— Panocha Eaters as they were known in the idioma, for now they ate little more than the gluey brown pudding made from wheat sprouted, dried and then ground into flour.

At nights, for she could be trusted, a neighboring Hermano came to visit Onesimo. He too was a simple, poor paisano and

had the Light in his eyes. In the dark he would knock softly
at the hut, and Onesimo would open the door.

"Who gives light to this house?"

"Jesus."

"Who fills it with joy?"

"Mary."

"Who preserves it with faith?"

"Joseph."

Thus they talked: catechism and answer. Then the visitor
entered. He bought an old paper book of faded writing. Its
leaves were tattered as if a goat had fed upon the edges. It
was a book of hymns; and because Onesimo could not read,
the rezador was teaching him the chants. The two men sat in
the corner huddled over a candle. Verse after verse the words
went on:

> *In these arms outstretched*
> *Here is the Divine Light!*
> *In His brotherhood we take*
> *Our Father Jesus . . . .*
>
> *De la tierra fui formado,*
> *La tierra me a de comer;*
> *La tierra me a sustantado,*
> *Y al fin yo tierra ha de ser.*

On Ash Wednesday, Onesimo climbed the hills for a piece
of flint which he chipped and sharpened. That evening as he
left the house he asked solemnly, "You will have a bit of
Romero Weed boiled for me when I return?"

Maria nodded silently and watched his tall lean figure,
head upraised, striding swiftly across the campo. It was dusk.
The blue mountain peaks were topped with snow. Up the
cañon, on a bleak water-gashed hilltop, stood a squat
windowless adobe. Before it rose a cross. It was tall and lean.
It looked like a man with arms outstretched. Quickly, before

dark, she went out for a bit of the weed.

It was boiled when Onesimo returned. Hearing his stumble, Maria lighted the candle. His face was more sallow, his eyes brighter. He lay down on the sheepskin, lifted his bloody shirt. There were three gashes down, and three gashes across his back.

"What is this?" she asked quietly.

"It is the thing of obligation," he answered softly.

So in silence she washed him with tea of the weed.

The Lenten penance had begun. For weeks it continued. Onesimo stumbled home with three lashes from a yucca whip on each side of his spine.

"What now is this, Onesimo?"

"For the love of God, the Three Meditations of the Passion of Our Lord." He would say no more.

Thus successively he stumbled home with the Five Wounds of Christ, and the Seven Last Words, and lay uncomplaining while she washed him with the rosemary.

But one night they brought him home on a burro. Two stern-faced, sad-eyed men held up his long, wilting body. They stretched him on the floor. His back was raw, the wounds of the lashes tangled like goat hairs. This, for the love of God, was the Forty Days in the Wilderness.

"I fainted. I could stand but few. My sinful flesh was weak," moaned Onesimo with shame.

"But his will be the glory," said one of the men, and they stood with unfathomable respect and pity in their dark, sad eyes.

Maria did not speak. Neither did she weep. But her heart bled like his back. And as before, she bathed his wounds with rosemary. What is the strange love of a woman to the stranger lover of a God? What is the meek rich ripeness of the earth to the brilliant blinding light? So in her misery she doubted the enduring even while she endured.

When a stranger happened to inquire why Onesimo was in bed that next day, she replied casually, "Why, Señor, that cranky old mule kicked him in the leg. He will soon be up, and with a club in his hand." But she did not invite him in.

At the beginning of Holy Week the two priests from the church rode up the valley. They went from hut to hut, from ranchito to ranchito. By the time they arrived at Maria's their scowls were black. But they affected a pleasant greeting, asked for water.

"Ah, you have not come to be married! You wish to live in evil yet, perhaps?"

"No, Señor Padre."

"Good! We will talk to your man about it. We will talk about the services to be held soon, on Holy Thursday, on Good Friday, on Sunday when the Christ rose again. You are coming no doubt?"

"Oh doubtless, Señor Padre."

"But where is your man?"

"Oh, he has gone up into the mountains for wood."

"But we see much wood behind the house."

"One always cuts wood."

The fat padre bit his lip. "I see no man in the fields. I see only women. Are they all cutting wood?"

"Oh doubtless, Señor Padre." And Maria watched them ride away, scowling.

Onesimo was gone all week. He was up at the morada, on the water-gashed hilltop up the cañon. She took her turn with other women carrying up bowls of panocha, sometimes a bowl of sopa. The walls of the morada were four feet thick, it had no windows and its one door was closed. She could hear chanting or praying inside. So she set her bowl outside and trudged back down the trail.

On Wednesday a light snow fell. Late afternoon the sun came out. The sky was gray, the earth was gray and bitter as salt. The morada on the hilltop squatted before the dark pines. Its cross spread its lean arms against the sky. From it at twilight Maria watched a line of men emerge and file up the cañon. She could hear, faintly, the thin piping of a flute and the low soughing of a chant. Several of the tiny figures were bent under crosses they were carrying. The rest swung their arms over one shoulder and then the other. She knew they were swinging braided yucca whips, beating their backs.

On Holy Thursday she saw them again from the door of her hut, her heart bleeding like Onesimo's back. "Pobrecito. Pobrecito." And she gathered still more rosemary against his return.

On Good Friday she awakened early, and with a premonition of evil. She bundled Niña on her back, and yanked Teodosio up the arroyo behind the house. They climbed higher—to the tall jutting cliffs above her old deserted mountainside hut. Across the valley she could see the squat morada. The brilliant blinding light beat down upon the snowy hilltop. The faded white cross gleamed nakedly against the pines. The earth was still, and the stillness was oppressive with the sin of man.

Again the procession came out of the morada, climbing into the dark cañon—the Procession de Sangre. Maria could hear no chanting alabados, could see no carried crosses. Just a long file of tiny men naked to the waist and steadily flogging themselves in silence. An hour later they came back and shut themselves up in the morada.

Far down the crescent valley, in Santa Gertrudes church bells began to ring. The roads filled with people dressed up in Sunday clothes for the padre's mass. Maria looked up at the sun. It was high noon. It was the time when the Three Hours' Services began, commemorating Christ's agony and death on the Holy Cross.

A flock of black shadows raced south over the snowy fields without cawing. A buzzard hung overhead. Maria shuddered. The silence thickened. Through it she fled swiftly back down the rocky trail, and shut herself up in the hut with the children.

Onesimo's faith gripped her by the throat. She lay down on her bed, and put her hands over her eyes to shut out the red marks on Onesimo's back of the Three Meditations of the Passion of Our Lord, the Five Wounds of Christ, the Seven Last Words, and the Forty Days in the Wilderness.

"Madre de Dios!" she whimpered. "What now?"

She tried to sleep.

The room seemed bare, dark and silent. It was neither. A narrow slit high up under the eaves let in a bit of strong, white, north light upon the white-washed back wall. Candle-light illumined the altar in front—a plank table covered by a dirty white cloth on which was sewn a row of huge black crosses. On it, besides the dripping candles, stood several wooden Santos: a large sad Cristo in lace petticoats; a smaller one naked and bloody with clotted red paint, and hanging to a cross; figures of the Virgin, of San Juan Bautista and San José. Before them lay an earthen bowl of flowers, a Bible and an old copybook of hymns, both opened. On the hard dirt floor knelt some twenty-five men. Their hierophantic bodies and low voices, the garish altar and weeping candles did not fill the room's sepulchral emptiness. They were part of it.

After a time the praying ceased. The phalanx of kneeling men became a wedge driven between death and silence, and life and light. Tears ran down their strong simple faces. Their brown bare backs were dark with clotted blood. Anguish dug their mudshoed feet deeper into the dirt floor.

The life and light came from a calm-faced, broad-shouldered man in the candlelight who began to read out of a book on the altar. He was the Hermano Mayor reciting the last of the Passion.

The death and silence was embodied in a man who knelt at the back of the room under the slit of white north light. His long thin body was naked except for a loin cloth. His arms hung limply at his sides. His lean ascetic face was tilted upward and sloped back from a weak chin to a narrow forehead. Neither his lips nor eyes moved. He simply stared, with a hypnotic look of gentle adoration and somber fatalism, at a figure on the right wall.

It hung by a cord around the throat, and with the terrible broken limpness of a body dashed down on rocks from a great height. It was dressed in rusty black cloth and small child's shoes. From its pale white head drooping forward, gawked huge, round, black eyesockets. In its limp, skeleton hands dangled a bow and arrow. It was a figure of Death.

The recitation ended. With a clear, sound voice the resolute, broad-shouldered man prayed God to forgive the sins of all the men in this world. The kneeling phalanx rose, sobbing. One of the men took the large sad Cristo in his arms, another picked up the open copy-book from the altar.

The almost-naked, lean ascetic still knelt in the back of the room as if in a trance. A compañero touched him gently on the arm.

"Brother. The time has come."

The tall, lean man rose and smiled. He followed the others outside.

Below the water-gashed hilltop lay the long, crescent valley. The late afternoon sun, like candlelight, gave it life. The snow had melted. The new plowed fields smelt rich and pregnant. The stream gushed noisily down the rocks.

But the wall of mountains above the morada was slate blue under leaden clouds. It shut off the sun from arroyo and piñon slope. A cold white light filtered through the pines upon patches of snow. The cañon was a dark mouth that swallowed a narrow trail. It held death and silence.

To it the men turned after locking the door of the morada. They formed a long procession which crawled up the narrow rocky trail into the cañon. The broad-shouldered man carrying the Cristo. The reader carrying the opened copy-book, and leading the hymn. The lean ascetic staggering under a heavy cross. And the rest, following behind, chanting and flogging themselves with whips.

Their deep male voices rose and fell in a monotonous miserere. So did the yucca whips—over one shoulder and then the other. Soon the sharp slap of the cactus on their backs became a soggy thud.

They kept climbing steadily but slowly. The lean ascetic with his cross retarded their progress. The leg of the huge, hand-hewn timber dragged on the ground. One arm stuck up vertically into the sky. The man's thin body bent under its weight. His sallow face flushed with exertion. Sweat ran down his gaunt cheeks.

He fell often: sliding in the mud at the bottom of the arroyo, stumbling over rocks as the trail rose upward, and slipping in the soft snow above. Face down he plunged, arms outspread, the heavy timber on top of him. For a moment he lay quietly, his breath whistling through the thin lips fixed in their unalterable smile.

His companions waited patiently, drawing their soggy yucca lashes through calloused hands. When the cross bearer had struggled erect they moved on, chanting. The snow banks ahead grew deeper, whiter. Behind, on each side, they were flecked with spots of red.

The trail led up into a small clearing behind the ridge of the cañon. Around it stood great serried pines and spruces. In it was a deep round hole. Here the line of men became a circle.

One of them stepped forward a pace with the sad-eyed Cristo in his arms. Another got down and dug out some fallen clods from the hole. Two others laid the huge cross on the ground, and bound the bearer upon it. Carefully now, and gently, they lifted the butt of the cross into the hole, tramped it solid and stepped back.

Over the ridge and down the cañon, spring had come to the valley with light and life. But here it was yet unresurrected winter. The pale white effulgence, without source, made a well of light in the dark forest. The bitter, pungent smell of leaf mold and soggy brown pine needles exuded death and decay. The great trees wept. Yellow tears hung on their bearded faces. The whole earth gave itself to the stark parable of the Crucifixion.

The man on the cross did not stir or whimper. His wrists and ankles were bound to the timbers with horsehair ropes. A dirty, white cloth band passing around his waist helped to hold him upright. Above it the ribs stuck out from his long, thin body. His lean, ascetic face was tilted backward against the beam. It still maintained a fixed and gentle smile. His dark eyes sought the heavens for an echo of his faith.

He was no longer a man. He was a great, obdurate fact—a fact timeless as the earth itself which ever dies to be resurrected again, the only enduring truth.

The outer circle of pines soughed faintly. The inner circle of men breathed hoarsely. And still he hung there, tossed up by the mute and unresistant earth, a hostage to the cruel and bitter skies.

But his long lean body had sagged. Little slivers of skin curled over the chafing horsehair ropes. His bony knees stuck out. After a time his head straightened. He was staring directly into the face of the Cristo held up to him.

There was something wrong about this face. It was a little too Spanish-Moorish with its sparse black beard carefully combed; and its sad eyes contained a bit too much resignation. This Cristo did not know that death of the earth which is a bitter thing and not accepted lightly. Nor did he know the terrible birth pangs of spring, that eternal resurrection which is a struggle worse than death.

But the man on the cross knew, being part of that earth so cruel and unresistant, so gentle and yet so enduring. And so his smile seemed slightly ironic and he closed his eyes as if the heavens were pitilessly empty of the faith he had sought.

Suddenly his head drooped forward. His body slumped, yanking at his fetters.

The circle around him broke. Men leapt to dig out and lower the cross, to untie him. The thing was over. They were no longer estatic Brothers. They were men with sore and bloody backs, half-starved from fasting on panocha. They began to talk, to shiver in the cold, to wind up their soggy yucca whips. Somber reasonableness came back into their tired, wild eyes.

A few drops of blood still splashed the sky above the pine tips, then night erased them with a gray hand. The men were gathered about the unconscious lean one untied from his cross and recumbent upon the ground. Lackadaisically they chafed his wrists and legs, waiting for him to come to. Now a fellow came up from the stream with water. He splashed it on the unconscious man's face, his wrists and belly.

Suddenly he stooped down. He stared at the ascetic, sallow face on which was engraven the gentle, bitter smile. He felt the thin wrists and let them drop stiffly back. And now, quickly, he bent an ear to the lean still torso.

"Mother of God!" he cried, jumping to his feet. "His eyes, his wrists, his heart—He. . . ."

The men surged forward.

"It cannot be! He is but young and frail. He is over weak from fasting. He lost too much blood for long. He spent his strength too freely. His faith has been too devout. . . ."

"Jesú Cristo! . . . God will not permit it! He has not permitted such a thing to happen for these many years!"

And still that great, obdurate fact lay there before them. Its lean nakedness was colder, whiter than snow in the shadow of the pines. Its deathly silence was more tumultuous than the thunderous mountain shapes. It was an immovable fact greater than their faith. In the chill darkness its wet loin cloth had already begun to stick to the damp ground.

The earth, of which he was a symbol, was already eager to take him back.

It was dark when Maria was awakened by a pounding on the door.

She sat up and stared, stupid with sleep, around the room. The knocking had stopped, but an echo still beat in her mind. It seemed an echo of something greater: of the hour after the

Christ had died upon His cross, when the heavens darkened, the earth gaped and the graves burst open.

Teodosio had fallen asleep on the floor, but Niña was pulling at her breasts and howling with hunger. It was this that finally aroused her.

She got up, lit candle and fire, laid out three bowls of warmed goat's milk.

Her mind had cleared now, but she still felt uneasy about Onesimo. Pues! He had always come back. He would tonight. Pobrecito, pobrecito. She set to boil a huge kettle of rosemary. Then she opened the door to stare out across the fields toward the morada on the water-gashed hilltop.

On the doorstep lay an empty pair of shoes. She closed the door and carried them into the candlelight. The shoes were old and shapeless, caked with mud and spotted with dried blood. They were Onesimo's.

The sudden meaning of their appalling emptiness stabbed her like a knife. It carved out her heart and bowels and mind. She stood more empty than the shoes, one hand clawing at her face, holding her breast, then pressing against her belly.

Teodosio and Niña were gulping goat's milk from wooden spoons. Maria bent down to her own bowl, and lifted out a hair from the milk with her forefinger. Suddenly she straightened. With a fearful howl she flung open the door and rushed out into the night.

5

Pues, there is this about all martyrs: the people they would have saved turn upon them and their memories alike, and the causes they die for grow cold and are forgotten. By their noble deaths they prove nothing but the supremacy of life with all its foibles. Even this Señor Jesús, the Cristo, and Onesimo who had died as He.

And Maria, lashing out against her anguish, banged His little cottonwood image over the fireplace, and cracked the Santo in two. She knew now exactly what Onesimo's death was worth to the people of the valley. At first the neighbors had given her commiseration, respect and help. Then slowly these changed to commination, fear and avoidance.

She heard talk.

"He was too young. . . . He was too weak. . . . His faith was not whole."

"What business had he to die? It is not the custom. Santísima! Now there is the devil to pay. All because of him. He foolishly let himself die, and so we must bear the anger of the priest and the curse of the church."

So, alone, Maria bent under the burden of their condemnation, the hunger of her fatherless children, and the niggardliness of her rocky field. And between the people and the church drooped somber storm clouds of mistrust and fear and hate. It was not only Onesimo's death and the unsanctified Brothers of the Light, but everything that was wrong.

The people no longer lifted their hats to the padre riding through the fields; the padre no longer rode forth to meet sullen faces and silent lips. The masses were ill-attended and heavy with threat. The archbishop had come and ordered the padre to excommunicate all flagellants from the church. But who were these Penitent Brothers? No neighbor took off his shirt in front of another at the stream's edge lest his scars be seen. Few went to church, they did not get married, they did not take their children to be baptized. The priest thundered against the people, and the people muttered against the priest. And over all, house and field and valley, drooped lower the stifling storm clouds of mistrust and fear and hate. . . .

Maria did not know why she went to church that day. She did not know why her neighbors went, nor did they. But there was something in the air—something light and fleeting that flew from ear to ear; something heavy and stifling that compressed people out of the cañons, and drew them to the church.

Inside, all was as she had seen it before; the honey-colored vigas gleaming in candlelight, the Santos and gilded crosses, the magnificent altar. She listened to the songs, smelled the fragrant little pot paraded around the room, watched the incomprehensible ritual of the mass.

But it was not as Maria had felt it before. For now, with bitterness in her own heart, she felt the distrust and fear and hate that oozed out from the hearts around her. It came through their taut heavy bodies as through fissures in the earth. It tinctured the air like the cloying odor of perspiration, like fumes of poison. They crowded about her, these hundreds of villagers and valley folk, with faces fixed and timeless as weathered rock, with faces dark and hard as hers. They waited.

Through candlelight and silence, the old fat padre came and stood before them. No sound greeted him. Not an eyelid fluttered before him. Yet before their stifling negation the priest went through his ritual. His stiff blue lips mumbled. His trembling white hands crossed and recrossed. He slumped to his knees and rose unsteadily. And now he was standing before them, and holding a little glass of Christ's blood.

"Padre! Oh my padre! Stop!" A woman's shriek rent the silence with frightened wings. It soared up to the timbered ceiling and raced frantically around the walls. "Stop! For the love of God! The sacramental wine. It is poisoned!"

The room erupted. It moaned, groaned, hissed, shouted, shook. It wept. The priest lifted his hand, and the volcano of noise and movement ceased.

Now he held up the little glass. It did not tremble, nor the hand which held it. His legs were no longer weak. Firmness smoothed out his white face. Strength parted his blue lips in a gentle smile.

Maria, watching him, felt the bitterness gush from her heart. Hot drops of anguish rolled down and cooled her cheeks. He was no longer the hated padre. He was something more. It came out of his voice.

"My children, my children whom I love," he said clearly, strongly, kindly. "The wine is poisoned, that I know. Yet it is wine of man poisoned by the hand of man, and so I know it not. For it has been blessed, and so it is no longer wine. It is the blood of the Christ which will redeem us. Shall we refute our faith in a moment of weakness? No, my children. This is my cup. In the name of the Christ who redeemed us with His blood, I cannot refuse it."

Wonderful words he spoke, smiling his sweet kind smile. He implored their forgiveness, forgave them their sins and the cup in his hand, entrusted them to the hands of God, these His children and his. So he prayed, standing there strong in his faith, kind and gentle.

And at its end, very simply, he drained the cup of poisoned wine. . . .

The padre's death lifted the storm clouds of mistrust and fear and hate from the land, and the bitterness and anguish from Maria's heart. She patched together the Santo she had broken, covered him with fresh yeso, and stuck him up in his old niche. But only as something Onesimo had treasured greatly.

Strange the faiths of men! Onesimo and the padre, enemies, had both died in His name, and their deaths had proved nothing but the strength of their own faiths. And now together in the same earth they lay silent: the padre in the Campo Santo, and Onesimo up the cañon above the water-gashed hillside.

> *De la tierra fui formado,*
> *La tierra me a de comer;*
> *La tierra me a sustantado,*
> *Y al fin yo tierra ha de ser.*

Long after the memory of Onesimo began at last to fade, she remembered this one of the many alabados he had learned. And to the earth, the living earth which alone would endure, Maria turned again.

She sold Onesimo's last mule and the pig, traded off the few sound sticks of furniture. She lugged rocks from the field, pulled up weeds, carried water by the bucket to the scrawny corn rows. Quelites, the wild greens, she fed her children, with milk and cheese from her goats. From dawn-dusk to dark she worked, and it was not enough.

The little crop withered without water, then a late rain washed the stunted stalks down the rocky hillside. The house was stripped of everything but a few pots, a heap of blankets, and two straw mats. Teodosio and the Niña's bellies were empty, like the house, and so was Maria's heart. By winter the emptiness began to show in her eyes. They were the mouths of two black caves that no one entered, an appalling vacuousness that wind nor rain nor snow ever filled.

Sometimes in the wintry twilight the villagers saw her coming across the fields. She stood at the door, unbending from the storm. One numb brown hand threw back the black shawl from her face. The other offered a cake of cheese for trade. And when she left with a bit of corn, they watched her stop furtively at the corral to gather up a handful of straw.

"It is that strange Maria," they would say. "The one with the evil eye. That woman and her goats! She would steal anything."

At dusk she reached home. Inside her rebozo she carried an armful of straw for her goats which she let into the kitchen. She raked up the fire on the hearth, stirred some corn meal into hot milk. Fed, the children fell asleep. Maria huddled before the fire, staring at her drowsy goats. Their wrinkled horns and skulls contained the only ineradicable record of this day's storm, this day's despair and victory—the infinitesimal mark of time, and the almost imperceptible warping of eternity. Their shagging pink-lit faces showed nothing of the change. They were the faces of philosophers. Maria understood them. She had accomplished the day. It was a victory. She slept without turning over, without a dream.

Winter passed, and spring and summer. Through them she fought her way from tortilla to tortilla, from meal to meal. She combated time with time's only weapon—the thrusting moment. Slowly she won her way through the years.

She did not try to plant and harvest the rocky hillside. She made the valley pay. At harvest she followed the falling crops. Where the wheat grew thickest, the oats tallest, where the corn drooped heaviest—there trudged Maria with Teodosio.

"Señor. Por favor. For the love of God, Señor. You will let me glean behind you? I have your permission, no?"

"Of course, poor woman! Would Fulgencio Garcia y Valdes have it said of him that he denied to the poor the gleaning of his fields? There along the acequia in the mud. There close to the chokecherry thicket where it is difficult to swing a blade. A fine stand it is! Almost a row!"

So by day Maria rivaled the crows, and by night she rivaled the stray stock loosed in the fields according to custom. Her reward was blanketfuls of grain hid in the thickets and brought home at night. Her own feet, Niña's and Teodosio's and those of her goats threshed it on the bare floor. She separated it carefully: the small wrinkled grains and the nubbins to be eaten, the fine full grains and fat kernels to be packed and hidden, never touched by hunger.

In early spring she made the rounds.

"Señor, you are breaking this new field. It has never been broken before. It is a good field. It needs fine seed. The best. That I have. A little but the best. You would like to look at it, verdad? But a moment it takes to look."

"Ah, compadre! What talk I hear you make in the tienda! That you are short of seed when the earth cries for renewal. That you would buy seed brought across the mountains by strangers. Verguenza! Is that the custom nowadays? Is it that the good earth no longer cries for its own seed, that a mother would no longer suckle her own? Compadre. You remember last year's wheat? The great yellow grains, how firm they were, how they gleamed in the sun, the weight .of them in your hand! Five measures of them I have saved for you. What do you say to that, compadre?"

But not a fanega would she sell, not a handful. Two measures in the fall for one in spring. That was her price. Two measures of the best. She would pick them out herself.

Maria was wise and shrewd. From the cliffs of Los Alamitos to the flatlands below La Cueva, from valley wall to valley wall, she doled out her seed. Not to men living too close together, nor much to each.

She was also niggardly. For as the grain bags heaped she hid them beneath straw, secreted them in the loft, and concealed even in her goat's hut. She became known not for much, but for a bag or two that was always available. Of the best. She had a power, this stange Maria, even with seeds.

The Niña grew, and was a great help. Teodosio grew, but was never much. Maria bought a buggy and a pair of sway-backed skeletons covered with leather to draw it. In this she made him drive her all about the valley to deliver and collect her grain. She went north into the mountains where the snowy peaks rose out of pines, westward up the steep cañons where summer lingers but a month, south to the dry plains, and east. She began, twice a year, to cross the pass to the little settlements beyond the valley's rim.

The beautiful blue valley grew and prospered. So did Maria. But it was she who became known. Maria from the valley. Maria del Valle. She became the valley. In her buggy she brought its sunstruck wheat, its ripe oats, the sturdy corn, its wrinkled peas and round barley, and the look of the rich ripe earth that bore them. In her eyes she brought its repellent remoteness.

Back to it from across the wall of mountains, from the river bottoms beyond, she brought great necklaces of scarlet chile that turned blood red and brittle hanging from her rafters. She brought tomatoes, the little sweet peaches, apricots, and melons, the low-country fruit and vegetables. And all these, in season, for a shrewd profit. Herbs she did not forget, both those that grew in the valley and those that grew without. In cans and boxes and bottles, tacked on the walls, hanging from the rafters and drying in the loft, was poleo for colic, oshá and yerba de manzo and topalquin to break a fever, cota for rheumatism, ruda for paralysis, canaigre for soft gums, yerba buena for pregnant brides and tequisquite for gas in the belly.

She knew the secret uses of weeds and kept them handy:

tumbleweed, horse weed, milkweed, frog weed, waco and wild marjoram. Brown grass she dried and bound, popote for brooms and popotito for brushes. The long dry stems of sunflowers she kept for lighting cigarettes from the fire.

Natural colors for spun wool she knew how to obtain, and how to make native dyes. Chamiso for yellow and the lichens for light orange; peach leaves and cedar bark for green; oak bark for wine; walnut hulls for brown; chokecherry roots and berries for purple; urine with cedar twigs for Indian red.

Foods she knew how to dry and preserve in the old way, the way of the poor who know neither sugar nor salt, the way of the hungry who watch each apple fall, chicos, posole, nixtamal, panocha; ribs dried in the sun, jerked beef, dried corn and squash and apples, green chile roasted, peeled and hung up to dry, quelites dried and stored in sacks to cook with meat or gravy.

All these foods and seeds, herbs and weeds that filled the house, and were hidden carefully, Maria herself used sparingly. Never meat when a taste in gravy would do as well; never an apple without a spot. Time and hunger she knew she could never vanquish. She was content to hold them at bay.

Yet it was not alone these things she sold and traded. It was the advice, instruction and power that went with them. For she never abandoned her goats and the wisdom derived from reading their skulls. An old he-goat she sold. Another died. Their skulls came back to sit with others upon her rafters. They were pages of a book she bound together year by year. They were a chronological record of the span of life that flowed past her. And sometimes she caught glimpses of its course ahead.

So slowly money began to come in. No one knew where it went. Teodosio was lazy and ragged, Niña industrious and ragged. Maria went around in her worn, rusty rebozo, and shoeless half the year. The occasional peso squeezed out of her for staples—for salt and thread and lime—seemed wrung from her very flesh. She was almost self-reliant, and she seemed quite content.

Like buffalo, the black-humped clouds stampeded over the ramparts of the valley. The thunder of their hoofs shook the sky-plain. From their locking horns leapt zigzags of fire.

Suddenly rain fell. Great warm drops hissed on the dry, dusty earth. Then slanting silver threads unraveled abruptly the whole texture of the shower. Within two hours the storm was spent.

A rainbow brilliantly colored as a Chihuahua serape hung over the shoulder of the sky. Pines and piñons glistened with water. The sharp smell of sage cut with a whetted edge. The black plowed fields began to steam. The whole earth seemed quickened, in heat, and straining at invisible bonds.

Maria with arms crossed stood at her window. She was holding her full and strangely aching breasts. Maturity had filled the hollows of her face. The sun, coming out again, enlivened the dull red underneath her brown cheeks. Her black eyes were no longer dead and empty; they were alive and restless. Her firm body had reached the softness of a ripe peach that waits to be plucked, to rot with decay or wither.

The devil take it! She whirled around and put on her shoes. She grabbed down her rebozo and hurried out of the house. Three o'clock in the afternoon. Quitting her work, her house, and going to town for no reason whatever. Mother of God! What gets into a woman?

What comes over the whole earth at times like this? Maria stopped and plunged her hands into the black steaming loam, crumpled the wet clods under her nose. In the pasture beyond, a roan stallion raced blindly and alone, tearing up the turf. The crows applauded insanely.

At the edge of town Maria stopped in the road. A bedraggled gray hen squawked past her and cowered against the fence. After her flapped a rusty rooster. He flew at her, screaming, drove her out of the weeds with beak and spurs. Before she could break away, he leapt upon her.

Maria stood watching. The gray hen squatted in a puddle without struggling, her wings half outspread, her head bent meekly forward. On her, his talons dug in her wet feathers, titillated the rusty rooster with his powerful, rocking tread. In a moment he stepped off daintily, shaking his feathers. He glared around haughtily, but with the fierceness gone out of him, and stalked away.

The little gray hen remained the victor. She chuckled over his betrayal, smoothing her ruffled wings and lifting her langorous yellow claws, one at a time, to shake free of mud. She looked smug and self-sufficient, as if the road had encircled the world to meet in her plump, bedraggled ball of feathers.

Maria went hot with anger. She stooped and threw handfuls of mud at the hen who only walked away disdainfully. "Cochina! Pig! Sorda hija de tal!" The hen threw a look and a cackle back over her shoulder, and ducked through the hedge. Maria, still steaming, walked angrily into town.

At Pierre Fortier's she banged back the door and stalked inside. Pierre left the men grouped at the stove and clumped to her on his wooden leg. "Ah, it is Maria! Whom I have not seen for these many weeks. You are well? And the children? And doubtless needing new supplies. . . .What a shower! I feel spring in my bones. It makes me hungry for life and meat. Fresh meat. Look! Behind, there in the corral, they are butchering. I have bought two steers. Look. A bit of fresh meat to take home for a change. Fresh beef from the mountaintop pastures. Maria. . . ."

Maria spit on the floor. "Beef! Santísima! You are talking to a poor old woman? An old woman who praises God when she can season the pot with a piece of goat flesh? Pagh! You and your talk!" She glared at the men crowding the stove. "Well, come and talk here at your desk, over your papers, about how much I owe you. Why you have cheated me, on paper, thinking my memory weak. Talk! Sí! It will take much talk."

It was as good as anything to vent the nervous excitement that had filled her veins—this long harangue over salt, sugar, thread, lime. Pierre, with spectacles on, sat his stool quarreling. Maria squinted at the fly-specked paper as if she could read. Neither was angry, neither misjudged the accuracy and shrewdness of the other.

At the end Pierre Fortier slapped his leg. "What a magnificent memory! The like I have never seen!"

"So that is what I owe?" mumbled Maria. "Well, it is good for both of us to know that when I have the money I shall pay. Certainly. But not now. Does silver grow on trees?"

Pierre reached behind him and took down a red cotton kerchief—the most faded and fly-specked of the dozen that hung on a rope. This he flung around Maria's neck and knotted. "A present. For my best customer. This most beautiful of all my fine scarfs. Madre! It makes you look like a girl! What beautiful red cheeks!"

Maria stamped her foot. "Fool! You think to shame me before all these men?" But she stole a look into a mirror, and swiftly reckoned the amount he would somewhere squeeze into her bill.

"Now. That fresh beef," Pierre reminded. "You will walk by the corral? You will see the fresh, firm red meat? Then you will return tomorrow for the piece I shall save?"

"I shall walk by," promised Maria at the door. "But no more. Am I a wealthy woman that I can eat beef like the rich and yet keep my friend waiting for his money?"

Pierre sighed. "It shall go on the paper. Do I not know my people?"

It was as he had said; in the corral just off the plaza the men had waited to slaughter until the shower was over. Maria leaned over the fence.

Two steers had already been killed. Dripping blood, they were hung up to be skinned. Two others waited their turn in a small corner enclosure. Their hoarse, frantic bellowing, the stark fear in their eyes, roused no pity in Maria.

The puddles in the corral seemed to reflect the sun lowering on the Sangre de Cristo. The mud itself was red and slimy. It seemed to give off a heat that crawled under her clothes. It smelled. The smell was aphrodisiacal. Maria's black eyes glittered. She loosed the red kerchief about her throat, and panted quick pale breaths into the cold afternoon. Crowding close against the fence, she kept rubbing her breasts back and forth over the top aspen rail.

Two men had come out of the log enclosure. One was a bearded old man in a leather coat who carried an axe. The other was a tall lean man naked to the waist, and carrying a long knife. His strong smooth back revealed long ropey muscles writhing under the skin. Maria sucked in her breath and shuddered as the hard tips of her breasts drew back over the rough bark. Then she pressed forward again upon the fence, the pink end of her tongue showing between her lips.

The bearded old man threw open the gate, stepped back and lifted his axe. As the frightened steer came out plunging, he swung once, twice. The blunt end of the axe thudded on the steer's forehead. He dropped to his knees.

Before he could roll over, the tall lean man stepped forward and drove up from his thigh the naked blade. He gave it a twist. From the steer's throat gushed a warm flow. It covered his knife, hand and wrist as he stepped back.

"Santána! What a steer!" he laughed, turning aorund and shaking his arm. "As full of juice as a ripe peach!"

Through a film of dizziness Maria could see the cold pink peaks, the corral filling with blood and its hot sweetish smell. She could see the man's chest now, hairless and sharply outlined as if carved out of wood, his flat muscular belly, the strong sharp lines of his jaw and cheekbones. He was laughing. His teeth gleamed white, like a wolf's.

Then, just as he turned around, he saw her. His look was dark and quick, sharp as a knife. It cut through the film over her eyes which dropped away like a curtain. It twisted; she opened to receive it, and something deep inside her gushed forth to meet his knifelike gaze.

A moment did it. Maria straightened, adjusted her new red kerchief, and moved a few paces along the fence. The man had stopped laughing. He was tense, impatient.

"Carajo!" he called to his companion as the steer was dragged away. "Why do you wait? The sun sinks. Let us have the other." But he kept glancing obliquely at Maria sauntering along the fence.

The last steer plunged out to meet axe and knife, to roll over sideways in blood and mud. The man stepped aside, drawing the blade between his bloody fingers. Maria had reached the end of the corral fence, and was walking demurely into the road.

"There!" he called loudly. "It is the last. I have bargained for no more. There is just time to return to the mountains before dark." He walked to a hollowed log trough and began to wash.

"But compadre," complained his bearded companion, "how is it you do not wait? A good drink to finish a nasty job. Has it not always been so?"

"Carajo!" sputtered the answer through cold rain water. "Am I a butcher, a meat carver, a shopkeeper? From the hills I delivered my beef. I killed them as was agreed. I go. Adiós. Adiós, compadre." He threw on shirt and jacket, saddled and rode out of the corral.

Maria was not a kilómetro up the road when he drew rein beside her.

"Cómo está, Señora?" he spoke in a voice soft as the dusk.

"Bien. Y usted?" she answered quietly.

But again the sharp dark look passed between them.

They walked along without speaking. Maria trudging along the side of the road, and the man jogging slowly beside her on his horse. He had put on his hat, and rode head down. His boot and trouser leg were stained with blood. The horse smelled it, threw up his head and twisted from side to side.

The leather squeaked. The bit jangled faintly.

When the tall cliffs jutted out, Maria turned aside without speaking. The man followed her up the lane on his mount. They stopped before the house.

"It is where I live," Maria said simply.

"You are the woman with the strange power," he answered in a deep, quiet voice. "Perhaps to this one you will bring luck?" And he stared down quietly from his saddle.

"Quien sabe?" she smiled. "Come."

He dismounted and followed her into the long back room. The dusk was thicker inside the hut. He could hardly see the rows of pale skulls, but the smell of drying herbs wrapped around him. He rolled a cigarette with fingers that trembled a little in the light of the narrow window. Then he sat down before her on a stack of sheepskins.

His breath was coming quicker now. His shirt front was open at the collar, and at each breath his smooth powerful chest swelled toward her.

Maria reached out and took his hands. She turned them palm up, squinting at the few lines etched into the firm calloused flesh. Their heads lowered, almost touched. Their breaths made one heat. Now Maria laid his hands in her lap. Her finger tips began to trace the lines up his corded wrist. From the touch little zigzags of fire leapt up his arms. Others leapt up her legs as he rubbed the backs of his hands over her knees. The room was darkening as with a storm. Its clouds flushed the cheeks of their bent heads. Abruptly he grabbed her by the wrists.

Maria stiffened, raised her head. From outside came the sound of wagon wheels and voices. The man drew back, wary, remote. Maria rose. She laid her hand on his warm throat, pulled his ear, then stalked to the door. Teodosio with Niña had just driven up in the buggy.

Shrieked Maria, "Sick pig of a litter! And you, lazy one! Can you not see there is one here to consult me? Are you blind to his horse tied there, that you would interrupt? Go!

Stay as you have stayed away all this day. Go to the tienda and there obtain the bit of fresh meat Pierre is saving me. Ungrateful children! Shameless ones! Go!"

When the wagon turned down the lane into the dark, Maria closed and latched the kitchen door. Then she walked swiftly into the long back room, taking off her new red kerchief.

Thus it was. A quick look from a man's eyes, the chance touch of a hand in the plaza, a meeting in the dark. They came unbidden, unlooked for, but with the imperative gestures of destiny to punctuate the monotone of Maria's life.

Later, heavy with child, she saw the man riding by into his cañon without stopping. She met another in town with his wife, and only nodded casually.

"What! Another child? And who this time can be the father?" she overheard, and Teodosio's answer, "Pues. Am I a son who is his mother's master? How is it that I should know these things—who is driven to work from dawn till dusk? It has happened before. What man can say it will not happen again?"

It mattered little. Maria accepted her nameless children as she had accepted the quick look of their fathers, the touch of a hand, the meeting in the dark, the beginning and end of the one enduring mystery.

They grew. Maria grew. They valley grew. It was all one rhythm, but with changing tempos like the seasons.

The French had disappeared, the fort had crumbled; the trappers and traders, the white-topped wagons came no more. The land was no longer Mexico but Nuevo Mexico. It was a Territorio of the east and not of the south. Now this was a strange thing, gringo land but no gringos. How was this, that the beautiful blue valley high in its sierras should remain untouched, unchanged by change? Because, Señores, the Jéfe, the gringo Presidente, loved his people here and wished them to retain their land.

They all filed down the trails to stare wonderingly at the
anunciados, at their great gold seals, and to hear the news
that the "Said claim known as the Demora Grant" had been
"recommended for confirmation by the United States Sur-
veyor General."

Bravo! Bravo, Señor Presidente! The land will be ours, as it
has always been. But whose?

Well, it is like this, compadres. The beautiful blue valley
will be divided under the eyes of the Presidente among those
seventy-six who came first to break its soil. But some have
died. Some have sons. It is true that these sons have sons. So
the land must be subdivided among all in the eyes of the
Presidente: to each his share, with a little piece of paper from
the Presidente, that hereafter there will be no quarrels.

And so the people stand in a long line before a man at a
big table covered with papers. He is a gringo with light hair.
He is one of the intelligent, wearing spectacles and holding a
pen. Under a flag he sits. He is, in fact, not a man. He is
authority. He is the right hand of the long arm of the Señor
Presidente. Beside him stands an interpreter.

The people present their claims. The right hand of the long
arm of the Señor Presidente writes swiftly.

We have lived on our land, we have loved it, we have
worked it, Señor. Myself, my father, my father's father. Now
I have this paper which says so and more—that it shall be my
son's and his son's. It is very well. Gracias, Señor. And to the
Señor Presidente, my devout respects.

The interpreter duly translates. The man bows, steps back
humbly, hat in hand. Next!

But there are difficulties, there are squabbles.

You see, Señor, this land is very old. It is not measured in
acres. It is not parceled in squares of meadow, of grazing
land, of mountain slope. For then it would be unfair. It runs
in the old way, in strips, "from the river to the mountain
top" or "from mountain top to mountain top" across the
valley. In this way, each man has a bit of meadow to plow for

corn, a bit of pasture for his cows, a bit of forest for wood.
The vara is the measure, Señor.

The Devil!

The vara, Señor, is thirty-three inches.

The Devil, I say! What is this, a strip three varas wide? Are
they crazy, to work land scarce nine feet wide?

It is this way, Señor. A man takes an equal share with his
neighbor when the land is new and plentiful. But should he
hold it when he cannot work it? The land must be worked,
Señor.

Or again. A man has six sons. He dies. To each he leaves a
strip, perhaps twelve varas, perhaps less. From mountain top
to mountain top. So that each shall have a bit of meadow, of
grazing land, of forest for wood and vigas and fences. Is it not
reasonable, Señor?

So it goes on for hours, for days. And each man goes out
with his piece of paper. And the ownership of the valley is
slowly confirmed, officially, as the Señor Presidente wishes.

Now comes a woman, shoeless, in a rusty black rebozo.
With her stands a listless, loose mouthed man with his fly
unbuttoned, a ragged haired girl and three small children. She
is greedy for land, for papers to the tall cliffs jutting out into
the valley's throat, for the forest slopes above and the vegas
below. But certainly she has a right. She is one of the first
settlers in the valley, her man was son of another. She has
lived on the land, no one has denied her claim, it is the will of
God. . . .

Come, come. Let's get at the root of this. Methodically.

"The Devil! Doesn't she have a name? Ask her what her
husband's name was," the man at the desk demands of the
interpreter.

"Maria of the valley. Thus only she is known."

"Maria del Valle! Why didn't you say so!"

Well, yes. But no. This woman had no husband; she has
never been legally married.

"It is often the custom," advises the interpreter. "Marriage by God and not by church. There are no illegitimate children; they are 'natural' children."

So! And Teodosio, this long lazy one with his fly unbuttoned, and Niña here with straggling hair go down on paper for the strip of land which is the share of one Onesimo, their father.

But what about another strip, the share of Maria and these other three children?

The Devil! All these children and no fathers at all! All right, all right. Not that it matters, a few minors' names scribbled on a paper. "But what do you call them? This one?" He jerks a thumb at the next oldest boy.

Maria recollects. His father came from San Antonio in the upper end of the valley. "His name, Señor, is Antonio."

"Antonio what?"

Well, thinks Maria, he watches the cow in the pasture. "Antonia de la Vega."

And this girl whose father lives in Santa Gertrudes. Will she not be able to help with the crops, such a quick hand?

"Gertrudes Paiz."

Ah. But this little barefoot chamaco, wild as a deer. Maria smiles. That was passion! The hot leaping blood, the quick moment under the willows, and then receding hoof beats of a horse bearing his rider to refuge in the mountains.

"His name, Señores, shall be Refugio Montes."

Thus it was, "In witness whereof, I, Ulysses S. Grant, President of the United States of America, have caused these titles to be made patent, and the seal of the General Land Office to be hereunto affixed."

And Maria stalked out with her papers. She had her strip of land from the tall weathered cliffs, across the valley to the pine hills. And her children, priest or no, had proper names, on paper. Bonita! Qué bonita! Such pretty names. Yet who shall know their fathers—as if it mattered?

Maria sighed satisfaction. It was a good day's work. That night she allowed herself a cup of chocolate, and permitted Refugio Montes del Valle to lick out the mug.

6

Maria at fifty was short and shapeless, her skin dark, dry and wrinkled. She was like the talus slope behind her house, the decomposed granite eroded from the cliffs, integrated by weather and weight, and now congealing into stone again. She looked juiceless, settled—and at any moment was likely to come roaring down with invective into the valley. To vecinos and townspeople she was a power and an enigma, to her children a despot. All called her Doña Maria.

To escape her tyranny, Refugio Montes took to his heels into the mountains. Maria sighed, erected a little wooden cross to his name in the Campo Santo, and appropriated the land due him at age. Antonio de la Vega she allowed to marry and build a hut in the pasture; as tribute he took care of her cows and goats, and his wife supplied her with cheese. The Niña had borne somebody's child. Little Gertrudes Paiz helped nurse it to free Niña for work in the fields, and Maria bossed both. These three women and Teodosio comprised the happy family that crowded Maria's small adobe.

"And now! Mother of God! You would bring yet another

to spit upon the hearth!" she attacked him vigorously.

"Cómo no? Marriage is a man's fate. I have escaped it long enough."

There was in Teodosio's voice the smug assurance of a weakling who at last has found someone weaker than he. Maria looked over with amazement his long skeleton covered by a spotted suit with the fly open, his sallow, saturnine face. Her small black pig-eyes snapped.

"A man's fate! Carajo! You sick pig of a litter, who thinks himself a man. You who do nothing but drive half asleep from road to road. Who will drive me now when you have a wife cackling at your heels? Pig! Lazy one! Listen! Tomorrow you will begin a new house. There in the orchard, there along the stream. Then we will see about this marriage."

Teodosio sighed and rolled a cigarette.

Maria snorted and took it from him.

In three months the adobe walls were up; the vigas laid, thatched with aspen latillas and covered with earth; the dirt floor hardened with goat's blood. The new hut had one room, one door and no windows, and faced the house.

"There. It is finished. I shall be married before the first frost. On the dia de San Francisco de Asis." It was the only time that Teodosio had ever worked. He swelled with pride at his new house.

"It is not bad. It will do. But I expect the fireplace to smoke," said Maria quietly. "Now before you bring this ignorant rabbit of a wife home, where Niña can teach her properly how to live according to custom, you must move my things into this small humble hut. Thus you will enjoy happiness in privacy; while I, myself, will yet be close enough to keep an eye on all matters."

Teodosio, still sullen after two weeks sulking, brought his new wife home to live in the privacy of two rooms shared with Gertrudes, Niña and her child. The bride's name was Concha. She was small, big eyed and timid as a rabbit, café con leche in color, deeply pock marked, and with thick black hair drawn back over her small round head. She lived there two years. She was never much use in the fields: her back was too thin, and her feet never out of the squeaky, glass button shoes she had been married in—the symbol of village gentility. But she built fires and cooked, took care of Gertrudes and Niña's child, ran errands, fed Teodosio's team, plastered the walls in summer and scraped the snow off in winter, cut wood and tanned hides. All very awkwardly, said Maria.

She died not from too much happiness, according to Teodosio; nor to escape work, according to Maria; but to flee the everpresent specter of Maria looming suddenly in the doorway.

"Concha! In God's name! Here in this doorway, behind you, I have stood for three minutes. You did not hear me on the path for I have no squeaky shoes, useless on such a warm day. But here I watched. I saw you put on the beans, the sopa. All without making the sign of the cross on top. How then do you expect success and flavor?

"Yesterday, unobserved, I saw you clumsily bruise your foot while cutting wood. I came over. I saw you washing it in warm water to take away the pain. Imagine! I did not see you lay that silver knife upon the bruise, which would have healed it according to custom. No! You do not know. You do not remember. You are a task."

So Concha mortally fled the omnipresent specter of Maria. It was omniscient as well.

She would appear suddenly at a remote mountainside hut, and stalk in without greeting.

"You are Crescenciana, wife of Filadelphio Aleman, whose newest child is backward in talking and walking as well," she would accuse the woman sternly. "What! have you no eyes to observe those natural facilities of bird and beast which can be transferred to ailing child with the proper remedies? Listen well. Rub the child's legs with rabbit grease daily; it will impart life to lazy limbs. To induce talking give him to drink of the water left out overnight for the chickens. Take heed. . . . Now when the crops are gathered, and this backwardness has been overcome by following my advice, I would have for a present a fanega of that barley your man has planted. To Maria at the bottom of the cliffs in the valley you will send Filadelphio with it. Without fail. Understand?"

"Si', Si', Doña Maria. Gracias. Mil gracias, Señora." And the woman would watch her climb into the buggy beside Teodosio, and vanish down the cañon.

To other huts Maria went. To advise that the fingernails of a tiny babe should be torn off, not cut, lest the child be tongue-tied. If it were ill with the mollera—if the soft spot on the head was sunken in and the beat of the heart could be felt by a hand upon it, she directed that it be cured by rubbing with breast milk mixed with a pinch of salt. Mal de cuerpo she cured, and recommended morubio for poultices on yagas, the sores of the flesh.

From spring till fall she traveled, from Monte Aplanado to La Jara, up La Cañada and across the Cebollitas. She inspected the crops and herds, gossiped with the Indian women as they all lay in the hot mud baths at El Alto de los Herreras, exchanged wit and wisdom for seeds and herbs throughout the valley and even behind its walls.

Teodosio continued to drive her in the buggy, grumbling.

"From dawn till dusk we travel. Our road has no end. My life is jolting away over these cursed roads. My kidneys are shattered. Now I must get out again."

"You are a sick pig without insides. Besides, now that you do not have the responsibility of caring for a wife, it is well that you be occupied in greater matters lest your grief overcome you."

Teodosio grunted assent to this mocking suspicion of grief. It was the only way he could force himself to believe he had had a wife.

In the winter Maria kept to her hut. She scraped and read her goat skulls, prepared herbs and seeds, concocted remedies, and kept her own strange calendar.

Three days after Christmas she went around to her neighbors, borrowing their most prized possessions. When they were not returned, two of the women trudged the snowy path to her hut and cautiously knocked.

"Señora, pardon the intrusion, but you will remember that shiny brass kettle you borrowed. It distresses my heart to remind you of this shiny brass kettle, Doña Maria, but my kitchen wails its absence."

" And that horsehair rope, Doña Maria. The one you got from my man who bids me return with it. Three days after Christmas it was. You remember?"

Doña Maria lighted a cigarette from the fire with a sunflower stalk. "I remember. See, there is the pot, there the rope. It was the Dia de los Inocentes. But you have forgotten. So now to get them back you must pay well."

"But we do not understand, Doña Maria. You will forgive our ignorance, but that is my pot which my kitchen wails. I have not forgotten."

"On the Dia de los Inocentes," answered Maria imperturbably, "one is permitted to borrow from his neighbors. When they say, 'pero no por inocente,' then it is a loan. But when they forget, proving themselves innocent of the custom, then they must pay to get these things back. It is the custom. Now that is not a bad pot. A little battered perhaps, but still useful. For it I must have a good price. And one also for the rope. Thus you will remember the old ways which are best, despite these changing times."

Even so, occasional valley folk traveled to her door.

"It is the first day of the new year, Doña Maria. As you know, we are poor, our crops have been poor. But even so we have brought this little present of turnips. Perhaps it is possible that you can tell us what the new year holds, whether our oats will spring forth sparsely or in abundance."

Maria nodded. "Leave the turnips and return before midnight with a handful of the oats you will plant in your field. In this little pot, at midnight, I will plant them. It will set in the window, a forecast of your crop. Thus you may ride by, day by day, and read your future for yourselves."

So her name grew, and her power. She was tolerated with fustian phrases, hated in whispers, and respected silently. Of all the valley she was the most surprised to receive a declaration of love.

Fulgencio Garcia y Valdes brought it himself. He drove the quarter-mile from his own fine place in his best buggy. The morning sunlight made golden statues of his matched chestnuts. His polished boots seemed copper pillars marching down the path through the apple trees to Maria's hut. When he took off his big sombrero, his thin hair gleamed silver.

"Todos Santos!" whispered Niña to Gertrudes and Teodosio peeking through the window of their house. "The man is made of money. What can Don Fulgencio wish of Doña Maria—this time of day?"

He stayed two minutes. When he drove away, they rushed out to Maria. She was still shoeless, on her knees and replastering the fireplace.

"What?" she asked, smacking a handful of wet adobe into a hole. "Señor Garcia has requested me to become his wife. . . . What!" she shouted, after a look at their faces. "Do you find it so strange as that? Get out! Can you not see I am plastering before the spring rains?"

Women have as many ages as moods. When it comes to marriage they have only one. Its costume is procrastination, and its masks are coyness, shyness, modesty, fear and pride.

"The Devil!" men echoed in stores, saloons, in town and throughout the valley. "I cannot understand why Maria does not make up her mind. She is wise and powerful, it is true. But neither young nor virginal. And Don Fulgencio as you know is the best catch in the valley."

"Verdad. Verdad," whispered the women. "But there may be many things to consider. She is shrewd. She will consider them all."

So they waited the union of the wise and powerful Maria, and the rich and powerful Garcia. Meanwhile he came twice weekly to sit under the apple trees and press his suit.

Fulgencio Garcia y Valdes was a fine name and a poor figure. He was small, withered and brittle as a dead twig. His face was sharp and sallow, his voice either curt or oily. He was a politician and seventy years old; he called himself sixty and "an agent of the Government." His virtues were a sound seat on a good horse, and the best piece of land in the valley.

It happened to be the largest, and it lay adjacent to Maria's at the mouth of the cañon. There were rich flat varas for planting, lush meadows, an orchard. But the landmark of the valley was his great stone and adobe water mill located at the turn of the river. Its huge burrs had been brought from France when the mill, under his father, had been built to grind on contract most of the grain for the fort. The run-off was used as an acequia madre, and by an ingenious irrigation system which engineers from Europe had come to study, watered his rich fields.

But now the elder Garcia was dead, the fort gone with its fat contracts. The mill still ground grain for the people of the beautiful blue valley, but only sporadically. There was a smaller, cheaper one north; and besides, something had happened to the water. It only flowed half the time. So Don Fulgencio was content to work his fields, to strut through public opinion and local politics, and boast of his chestnut horses and horse chestnuts—he owned the only tree of its kind in the valley.

For all his wealth and importance, he lived like a peon, with an old blind crone, his sister, and in the back of the mill.

"Don Fulgencio is a gentlemen of the old days," people would say proudly. "A true caballero. He keeps his horses in his house and lives elsewhere."

It was quite true. The long, beautiful adobe house, crumbling through the years, he used as his stable. Where all his money came from no one wondered. The Garcias had always had money. This is the advantage of a reputation, that it persists in giving one what one has not.

All this Maria pondered. To others she seemed shrewd and deliberate. She herself was simply perplexed.

"Why is it you would marry me, Don Fulgencio?" she asked him one afternoon.

Señor Garcia rose and bowed, hat in hand. "Doña Maria, from the fullness of my heart. From the respect I bear you."

"Sit down, sit down," Maria demanded. Then chewing on a blade of grass, she said simply, "Now, Señor, to me this is a strange thing. Me you have known for many years and never spoke. Me you knew when the spring of life rose in our veins. How is it that the fullness of your heart did not overflow to me then? Is it that the passion of your body now calls for this old wrinkled flesh which has received many men and given many children? That I cannot believe. Nor can I believe you would be much of a man yourself in bed nowadays, Fulgencio. Our blood is no longer hot, mi amigo."

Garcia slapped his thigh. "Madre! My manhood has never been questioned. But I grant what you say, Señora. The vile lusts of the flesh no longer possess me. The union of our bodies I do not desire. It is simply as I say: that I ask out of the great esteem and treasured respect that such a woman deserves."

Now this was a strange thing, almost unbelievable, and when next he came Maria asked him, "This marriage, Don Fulgencio. I cannot see what good it would do you. I have good land, it is true. But you have better and more. Besides a mill. I have influence perhaps, with certain herbs and wisdom. But you have the power of an agent of the Government. The new gringo government. There are many men who mark crosses on their votes as you direct."

"You observe clearly," he answered. "It is one of your uncounted virtues. A woman who observes clearly. Pues, you are a miracle! But see yet further. I have power from the

Government over men. You have power over the simple. Is it not fitting that we two unite and so give to all the united leadership they deserve? How proud they shall be—and I, my dearly esteemed Doña Maria! That I, Fulgencio Garcia y Valdes, have been given to wife that gracious and wise Doña Maria whom all know and love. I dream of it nightly. What do you say, Señora? What answer may I hasten away with?"

And still another week she questioned him.

"I have not forgotten to think about this matter which concerns us, my friend. I have remembered many things. I was a young ignorant girl of the hills. I wandered with my goats. It was your father's men, and you with great cruel stones, who chased us from grass during drought. I remember when my man Onesimo died. I had the Niña and Teodosio when they were small. We were poor, we were hungry. We had nothing at all. To you I went for permission to glean your fields. You gave me scarce enough, where only the reapers could not swing their blades. The years have come and the years have gone, and we have always been the same. You have been rich and I have been poor. You are of the Garcias, and I am of the people. Your power is of the Government, of politics, of important things understood only by the intelligent. And they are good, doubtless. But my power is that of the wisdom of the people who do not think, but feel. And that is good too.

"Now it seems to me," she went on slowly, "that these two powers are yet far apart, even in these changing times. The power of gringo ways and politics, of steel plows and papers to land and houses, that rests in you. And the power of the simple, of the old customs, of the earth and its herbs, of the stars and the seasons, the power of the blood that rests in me. Perhaps it is not possible for these two powers to unite. Perhaps it is not fitting that we try to unite them. Señor Garcia, I am a simple, old and nameless woman. I have never learned to write my name. Why is it that you would wish to marry me?"

Fulgencio Garcia y Valdes still insisted. His honor was at stake. Imagine! The honor of a Garcia with the only chestnut horses and horse chestnuts in the valley at the feet of a simple goat woman. People discussed it fully. Their sentiment swung to Garcia.

"True, she has a nice bit of land," they said, "but what can Don Fulgencio get from this marriage, with more? She is old, mean and shapeless. Perhaps he wants her to read goat skulls to him, and the future. . . . Not that he has much of it left," they added maliciously.

Garcia cast now his pride at Maria's feet.

"Questions, questions, questions! I can stand no more. Doña Maria, you look at an old lonely man. Without child, without friends, with no one but a shriveled blind magpie to keep him company. What is this talk of lust of the flesh, of power, of name and custom and wealth? We are no longer young. Let us grow together in our gentle age, and so be wise at last."

Maria sighed. She felt her heart at last understood him. "Come to me yet once more. In three days. I shall have your answer."

Yet when he returned, her tongue was still sharp. "Señor Garcia, you desire marriage with me without the passion of the flesh?"

"Pues. I would not have it known, but my passion has ebbed. You may sleep where you will, as though a virginal maid."

"You have your work, your mill and land, your power with the políticos. You understand that I too have my life, though a woman?"

"Goat skulls and herbs! I have never seen such a woman! But I shall be busy. I shall not interfere with your days. Though I shall be censored for it, no doubt," he added lamely.

"Well!" Maria frowned. "This is stranger than ever. I can think of no reason for your marriage but the question of land. But wait! I do not know what the new law says about a woman's land. I do not want yours, nor shall you have mine. Tell me. Should we be married, on paper, would you first write a paper, a Government paper, that to me my land remains?"

Señor Garcia blinked. "The strip of your land from the cliff tops across the valley to the mountains. The land of your Antonio and Niña, your worthless Teodosio's. All your land in this valley. And you shall have your paper, besides."

Maria took a deep breath. "Then, Señor Garcia, I can think of no reason why you should marry me. . . . Nor can I think of any why you should not. It must be as you say, that you are an old and lonely man, though rich, who needs a heart with tenderness and pity. Perhaps I can give it to you, Don Fulgencio. . . . You may set the day for Santána."

She rose. Suddenly, with a strange gesture of compassion, she drew his head upon her breast. "Imagine, Don Fulgencio! I have never been married!"

It was high noon. It was mid-summer. A long line of wagons, buggies, horsemen and pedestrians crawled down the wide road. The blinding sun muted the shriek of colored paper and ribbons. Thick swirls of dust tarnished the laughs and jokes. The procession smelled of perspiration and whisky. It was el Día de Santa Ana. It was Maria's wedding day.

She sat in the most dilapidated buggy of all, beside Teodosio in a new suit with the fly sprung open. Her short lumpy body bulged out a cream satin wedding gown for which Don Fulgencio had himself paid two hundred dollars. A high, jewelled, Spanish comb wobbled in her black coarse hair. Her cramped feet sweated in brown shoes with glass buttons. To her swart, indomitable face she held in stubby calloused fingers a tortoise shell fan to keep off the sun. She was staring down the road toward the crowded village plaza.

Herself at midnight she saw mounted on a plodding burro

and carrying a small child. In back, on the rump, another sat swathed against the cold. Leading them in front walked a tall lean man, one hand thrust inside his leather coat. His face was raised to the gritty December stars.

"Mother of God!" ejaculated Teodosio. "Has there ever been such a day and a wedding? Look at the plaza. Listen to the bells. They sound as beautiful as the pesos Don Fulgencio jingled to have them ring.

"'Roll me a cigarette," demanded Maria sharply. "It is not fitting that I do so. Besides, I forgot my tobacco."

For the third and last time in her life, she entered the church. Nothing was as it should have been. She was no longer poor, sinful and humble. The church no longer remembered the tall lean man on his shaggy burro, or Him he had looked like, the gentle Jesus. Like her it gleamed with the glory of Don Fulgencio's gold.

"Santána!" whispered Teodosio as they walked down the aisle. "What a wedding! It is better than a fiesta mass. The bells, that was ten pesos. Don Fulgencio told me himself. The organ, that is fifteen more. Look at the candlesticks and the candles—at a peso for each. Madre! Listen now at the voices of los cantores. Six pesos more. To say nothing of those for the priest and the holy water, the use of the church, the flowers, the Holy Book, and God knows what else. You are a lucky woman!"

At the altar waited Don Fulgencio. He looked as though he had been dragged out of his great carved chest at home, black velvet embroidered with coroded silver, a little wrinkled, scrawny and juiceless, but satisfied and smiling.

When the priest came out, the music stopped. They knelt and rose. The priest spoke and prayed. They were married. And now as they passed out, the bells began to ring again.

"Bravo! Bravo Don Fulgencio! Brava, Doña Maria! . . . Salud, Señor y Señora!"

Don Fulgencio took out his buckskin bag at the doorway and threw money to the people outside. He strutted into the bars to leave more money for drinks. Then he escorted Doña Maria to his buggy and whipped up his chestnuts.

All afternoon they sat at home in the dreary back room of the huge mill. Don Fulgencio's old blind sister sat with them entertaining guests. The room was large, gloomy and stuffed with furniture from the abandoned house. It smelled of dust and flour.

"What a fine old chest!" a guest would say, thumping the stiff leather. "And that comoda. I have never seen such carving. From the old days it came. Up the Chihuahua trail. Pues, but times are changing. Still, Doña Maria, you are now a Garcia. It is a long way from selling goat cheese. No? I congratulate you."

The old blind sister sat pouring wine unerringly from a dusty decanter. Don Fulgencio talked horses and politics, water and crops.

"Doña Maria," another would point out, "your new husband has shown you the pride of his life? The great horse chestnut just outside? Such a tree! The only one in the valley!"

By dark they had drifted away, whispering. "Mother of God! Did you ever see such a bride? In that dress! That old herb woman, that peddler of goat cheese. And now the Señora Garcia. Who would have imagined our Don Fulgencio would come to such a thing? But it is said among the simple that she has a power. No doubt she cast a spell upon him. Well, we shall see what he gets out of it."

Inside, bride and groom and chaperon sat quietly in candlelight. It was nearly eight o'clock. Don Fulgencio began to figure the costs of the wedding. "Two hundred dollars for that fine dress. Then the shoes. . . . I gave the priest too much, but he wanted more. . . . There was the dobles—rung before and after, el organo and singers as well, la agua bendita and all the candles—did you notice how quickly they were snuffed? To say nothing of money thrown to the poor, and left at the cantinas. . . . Well, I shall get many votes for all this, mark my words! But an excellent wedding, eh Doña Maria? You will remember I spared nothing. . . . And you have your paper?" It was clearly a tone of dismissal.

The old blind woman sat staring, stonily, from her filmed-over eyes. "Come. It is time for bed. The Señor retires at such an hour." She got up, opened the chest, and began to spread the couch with blankets.

"And where do you sleep, sister?" inquired Maria gently.

The woman nodded her head toward the cramped kitchen where she slept on the floor.

"Go then and sleep, sister!" demanded Maria sharply. "Who else shall prepare a man's bed but his wife?"

When the woman had gone, Maria smoothed down the couch. Don Fulgencio sulked. He looked a little frightened, like one who is likely to choke from too big a bite.

Maria knelt silently and took off his shoes. Then she grasped him by the shoulders, gently, as one holds a child.

"Don Fulgencio. You have forgotten, but I remember the words between us. You are a powerful man, but you have been womanless too long to know that a woman has a power too. My friend, in me is that power and more. There is in me gentleness and pity for you, for never till tonight have I been a wife properly, on paper. So to you I give it.

"Now I go home to sleep, as is proper between us. Adiós, my friend. We shall talk tomorrow."

Through the willows along the stream, around the cliffs she crept home. Carefully in the darkness lest she be seen and so disgrace Don Fulgencio.

In her hut she took off her cream satin wedding gown and glass button shoes, laid away her comb and fan. Shoeless, in her worn black cotton rebozo, whe crouched before a tiny fire built to keep away mosquitos. Between her knees she held a goat skull.

"What a strange marriage," she thought. "Who knows what it means? But there is something wrong in it that defies all my wisdom. What is it that Don Fulgencio would have had of me?"

Ay de mi! What an illusion that time is a moving flood. It changes the world and the hearts of men. But the beautiful blue valley and Maria do not change. They are like time itself, the one impregnable constant.

"And no wonder," people said of her. "She is not only too old to learn, but too simple to forget."

"She stayed long enough to put her spell upon him," said others. "What more do you ask?"

Thus they explained Maria's return to her hut. Their explanations condemned her. But her obduracy which prompted them aroused their secret respect. It is the respect with which one beats a stubborn burro.

Maria did not heed their talk. She was still perplexed as to what Don Fulgencio had wanted from their strange marriage.

A railroad had come through the plains below the beautiful blue valley. Crews were cutting timber for ties in the mountains above. The great logs were freighted through Santa Gertrudes. The valley supplied men, and the men with supplies.

"I have been thinking," Maria had said to her husband. "Business is good. Water is plentiful. You could run the mill every day. And that, it seems to me, is a very good thing. That you should run the mill and so supply with profit to yourself the flour for all these men."

Instead, Don Fulgencio dismissed the man he had and closed the mill entirely.

Yet another year and Maria suggested, "Don Fulgencio, the water has been scarce this year. Now when you wanted to marry me I suspected this, that the time of drought would come when your land, being below, would want for water; and that mine, lying at the mouth of the cañon, would yet receive the stream's flow. Wherefore I suspected reasonably that you wanted my land to protect the water for your mill and also your land. Now it is no more fitting that a man's land go dry while his wife's prospers, than that hers be despoiled for his. But still you do not ask. Is it because of pride, because of the paper I requested from you? Shall I not instruct the Master of the Ditch to share equally between us the water in the acequia according to custom?"

But Don Fulgencio would not clean out his ditches for water, not that year nor thereafter, and let his crops prosper or wither as they would.

Thus no money came from his mill, no money came from his crops. But still, from somewhere, money came to him for everything, for buying votes and buying whisky for more, for shiny store clothes and riding to the city on the train which passed far below the beautiful blue valley. No one thought anything of it. Pues! The Garcias had always had money. Besides, was he not a político and an agent of the Government? But money he began to have for loans on land, and for buying land to sell again. This disturbed Maria.

"Of what use is land if it be not worked?" she asked him. "For land is land. Like women, it exists only to bear. It is a law above any on paper."

"Madre!" he answered irritably. "What does a woman know of business? To me my business as a man. To you your herbs and goat skulls. Let us not interfere."

But soon he ceased going to the city. He gave up his politics. He grew older, scrawnier, more brittle. His chestnut horses faded to buckskin shadows turned loose to pasture. But he still carried horse chestnuts in his pockets, and took immeasurable pride in the great tree outside, near the bend in the river. It became an obsession. Not a hand would he allow to touch it, not a foot to approach it. Under it for hours he sat nursing a secret fear and smug satisfaction that gradually distorted his thin sharp face. It was the look of a miser sitting on his chest of gold. He became feeble and crusty. He became unbearable.

"Don Fulgencio," said Maria. "Ours has been a strange marriage. You did not desire to possess my body, being too old and manless, and myself without desire, so I have slept at home unknown to the neighbors. You did not desire my land, neither water for your own. I offered advice on business, consulted the stars, read herbs and skulls that you might act with success when the time was ripe. You refused it all.

" 'Surely then, Don Fulgencio spoke truth,' I said to myself. 'He is an old lonely man. Out of the fullness of his heart and the respect he bears me, he desires for his last years on this earth the help, gentleness and pity of a wife.'

"This have I given you. Each day I have come. I worked, talked, prepared food, besides. For what? To be ignored, to be treated like a blight? I, Maria of the Valley? No, Don Fulgencio. So I go to return no more, not knowing what you wanted in marriage with me. Adiós, Señor Garcia."

The old white-headed man looked up with a scowl. He saw vanish the last personal care and pity that anyone was to call from Maria. Like the land, she had been fruitful and enduring, ever waiting for a master. But can it plow itself, can it bear without care? Thenceforth, crusted over, she knit back together into an earth inimical and unbroken.

So she returned to her hut, resuming uninterrupted her long rides with Teodosio throughout the valley and into the enclosing mountains.

But once she stopped at Don Fulgencio's. The fields were full of weeds, the unpruned orchard sprouting suckers. The fences were falling. Crows were picking the eyes out of two buckskin covered skeletons in the broken corral. Under the great horse chesnut a little wizened man with white hair sat muttering to himself. He kept plucking handfuls of earth, letting the clods trickle from hand to hand like hoarded gold.

"Doña Maria! Keep away from this tree!" he screamed, leaping to his feet upon seeing her. "Away! Accursed woman, wife who is not a wife. You have laid a spell upon me!"

She walked into the mill. The machinery had rusted. The great wheel was broken. Green slime filled the sluices. Rats

still scampered through the empty bins. Cobwebs laced the
rafters. In the back room, in dust and silence, huddled the
old blind crone with her rebozo drawn up over her head.

"Maria? It is the steps of my brother's wife? You got my
message?"

"It is not your brother's wife. It is not her who got your
message and whose steps you hear. It is Maria. Maria of the
Valley who comes here as she would to any other place."

"Ay de mi, Doña Maria. You have lived to see fall the
house of Garcia. But to you in your simple wisdom, being
less talkative than others, there is something I would say
before I die. Go quietly and unseen into the back garden . At
the foot of the grandfather apple tree, the gnarled old one
with the low crotch seven paces from the crumbled wall, dig
and bring me the small box you find among its roots."

Maria obeyed.

"You found them? Here, let me feel. Yes, they are the
heavy gold pieces. The same. The old ones. Do you find them
tarnished, Doña Maria?"

"Not tarnished, but dull. Neither are they round, but
square," answered Maria.

"But still gold which remains constant in all it forms, and
thus invaluable to the greed of men," observed Maria.

"Pues. Take them. Bury them again where you will against
the hour of need—the hour of my death. For all their corners,
being gold as you say, the priest will not refuse them for
dobles, for holy water and el sepulchro. It is not fitting that a
Garcia, even a blind childless woman, be buried without the
sound of the bells, and a proper entierro. If there be enough
for a candle or two, so much the better. I have been in dark
long enough. You will do this? I can ask no one else."

"I will not refuse," agreed Maria. "Console yourself against
the hour."

"Well then!" spoke up the blind woman. "Listen now to
what I would say. It is your proper payment."

"You observe him sitting forever under his tree—he, my

brother, your husband in name? You heard him shout at you
in madness when you approached. You hear me now relate
how he beat me with a stick the day I went there to gather
dry twigs. Look at the bruises on my flesh, feel the welts on
my poor head, which still remain!

"Doña Maria, there are things to be said which one cannot
say. But you are a wise woman who can hold her tongue and
be patient. Do you not wonder how a man can be so rich and
yet so poor, and why he sits forever under a worthless tree?
Go then, and remember this box of gold pieces, myself and
him who guards an old tree not worth guarding of itself. In
these words and your remembrance of them lies your
reward. . . . Do not forget the candles! Being faithless you
can talk sharp business with the priest. One at the foot and
one at the head, if possible, Doña Maria. Do not forget."

For months a somber gray had overhung the valley,
blotting the beauty and obscuring the blue. Fall it was and
still raining—an incessantly dripping mist, a sparse quick
splatter or the lash of a heavy storm.

The earth was soggy. Adobe walls kept crumbling. Anemic,
water-logged corn straddled puddles. Beasts and birds of the
field dragged hoof and claw as if too discouraged to shake off
the clinging mud. When the sky appeared to be clearing, the
river bloated with more debris; there had been another heavy
rain up one of the tributary cañons.

"Mother of God!" a man would exclaim, tramping in from
the fields. "I have not seen it so wet in thirty years. For all I
feel it might be that long since I have seen the peaks against
the sky, the clouds lie so low and heavy."

Weeks ago when the crops were given up, Maria had put
away her goat skulls and marked willow twigs, had discon-
tinued watching for dry stars. She was a woman vigilant of
the future, not unaware of the past, but wise enough to give
herself to the present.

So she sat quietly in her hut, head down and listening to

the orchestration of the day's storm. She was cooking beans. The fire rubbed long red hairs against the pot. Its reflection lay like thin straw on the floor. Outside, the apple trees shivered; fruit thudded on the ground like lazy thumps of a drum. The rain on the roof was a pizzicato, the rumble of the creek a sustained adagio.

At mid-afternoon came a violent crescendo. A bit of roof dirt trickled down between the rafters, followed by a steady drip of water. Maria set a pot under it. Soon there were seven pots filling on the floor. "Diablo! A seven pot rain! One more than the worst!"

When the hard mud floor became sticky, Maria grew uneasy. She opened the door. It was scarce five o'clock but dark. The creek roared beyond the little orchard. A sour smell tainted the air. The rain was coming down, as it is said, in buckets. In the corral Maria saw lanterns.

"Teodosio!" she called. "What is the matter with you? It is a seven pot rain, and more, for I have none left. Come! Move my things into the house."

"What is the matter with you?" he shouted back. "We are carrying chickens into the house. We have lost two already. Are you blind? The corral is ankle-deep in water from the creek."

Maria grabbed up her rebozo, and went out. The little stream coming down the cañon was a torrent. At its junction with the creek, the water had banked up against the cliffs and was creeping through the orchard. Above, the wall of stones which protected the corral from the creek was hidden by water.

Hurriedly she lugged out armfuls of things from her hut. The house was already full of chickens, goats and a calf, Niña and her daughter, Gertrudes and Teodosio. The chickens picked at her seed corn, the calf nibbled at her precious herbs. The goats stared disconsolately at the heaped skulls of their predecessors. Gertrudes and Niña's girl examined her old clothes. Teodosio grumbled at the half-cooked pot of beans, and Niña at the weather. The rain clawed at the walls, trying to get at them all.

"These beans!" muttered Teodosio. "Not only are they half-cooked but full of water. Now I would not say you failed to put the lid on as you carried them through the rain. Carajo! You could make me believe it rained through the pot itself, so strongly it drives!"

Maria sat still, head cocked; there had sounded outside a queer splintering. "The hut," she said, rising, "it—" Even as she spoke came the crash.

They ran outside; the path was shin deep under water. Maria's hut had fallen down. Water had dissolved the lower bricks.

"Well!" shouted Teodosio. "Now you will be glad to go back to your beans, in warmth and comfort, be they half-cooked and cold! Our Lady! You moved out but in time!"

They trudged back. But not before Maria had looked long and anxiously up the cañon. It was raining harder than ever.

The roof of the house was the usual: large hand-hewn vigas laid across the tops of the walls, a cross-hatching of small aspens, on these a few planks, and covering all, two feet of dirt. By eight o'clock water had soaked through. Everyone and everything was wet.

"We are on a rise. The walls rest on stones. We are safe but miserable," observed Teodosio, with water running down his back. "But Madre mia! It is like trying to escape fate to dodge these trickles. Even my cigarette papers are wet. I do not have a dry pocket."

"Let us go down the road toward the village," pleaded Niña. "We shall come to a dry house. The beasts here will be safe. But I can stand no more."

Teodosio opened the door and stuck down a foot. He drew back a leg, wet to the knee. "Mother of God! Go? How? We should need a boat! But not this one. Why should he go outside to get wet? There is plenty of water in here."

Maria stood beside him, holding up the lantern. She was smelling the air.

"Come! I have a certain foreboding. But leave the doors open for the beasts." With this she plunged out into the night.

The others waded after her flickering lantern. Near the road they heard the splash of horses, saw the light of a torch. It shone on a bedraggled family down from the opposite side of the valley.

"Teodosio! And Doña Maria!" exclaimed the man when they met. "Thank God for such good neighbors. You look upon ruined friends. Our house has fallen in. And here you stand in water to meet us, and lead us to spend the night in your own warm house. In this storm we might never have found the way."

"Jesú Cristo" answered Teodosio. "You mean to tell us that water floods the north as it does the south? Us, who are washed out like rats, even as yourselves? Cristo, Cristo!"

All straggled on in wet and darkness. "Maldito!" cursed Teodosio. "Is this road or river? I can tell only what it once was by the fence posts."

They came to the house of Santiago Jacquez; it was dark and crumbling. They came to the house of Mechor Sandoval; it was deserted, the chairs were floating out. They reached the house where Quiteria Pacheco lived with her three sons, the ranchito of Fidencio Romaldo y Trujillo, the long adobe wherein lived the three poor families of Santistevan, Espinoza and Donaciano Romero. They were all abandoned and besieged by water. It was midnight and still raining when they saw a light.

"Ójala! I know it now!" exclaimed Teodosio. "It is that old stable of gray stone near the bridge. Across from the mill of Don Fulgencio. We have come not more than a kilómetro! Imagine! Pues. Are we ducks, are we fish? Come! I smell coffee and tortillas, a warm fire."

But inside were only Santiago, Mechor and Quiteria with

their wives and sons, Don Fidencio and the families of Santisteven, Espinoza and Romeros. There was no coffee, no tortillas. There was not even a fire; there was no dry wood. There was hardly room to squat down. "So this is what a man gets, swimming like a fish a kilómetro that seems ten leagues!" grumbled Teodosio. "Not even a dry cigarette."

One by one more groups splashed in to stand dripping in the light of torches. From Tramperos, Cañoncito, La Corriera.

"What! Is it raining there too? You brought no dry cigarettes? No?" Teodosio asked each.

No one answered. They were a people elaborately dumb under misery and misfortune. All watched Maria who kept opening the door to sniff the air. The light from her lantern flickered out to the watery fields. All the stock had been let loose. Horses, cows, burros, goats, pigs and sheep splashed round the building, whimpering.

An hour after daybreak Maria turned back from the door. "It is coming. What I feared and suspected. A new smell and fresh mud. The creek brings down not only wreckage and willows, but fresh pine tips. Come! We must go! To the village."

They straggled out again. The pallor of dawn was reflected in their muddy faces. Their features were set like cement against sleep and hunger, fear and misfortune. A child whimpered with cold, their only voice. Behind them splashed twenty head of loose stock. No one seemed to notice that the rain had ceased. For at the bridge the creek was still swelling.

They looked back. The valley was no longer beautiful and blue. It was gray and slimy. It smelled sour. They looked ahead, and it was the same, soggy fields crossed by rivers that had been roads, and sodden adobes from which no smoke rose. But there stood the church tower of Santa Gertrudes. Down to it from the southern slope of El Alto del Talco, from the northern slope of El Alto de los Herreras, plodded more people across the fields. And down the little mountain pass from La Cuesta, Ledoux and El Oro, from the Cebollita valley, trudged a steady line of people and stock.

But Maria was staring back up the crescent valley, at the tall cliffs near the curve and the shrouded mountains toward the north. A man had stuck a stick down in the creek bank. He came running back with it.

"Mira! Doña Maria, look! The water was here when I placed it. Now it is here. A good two inches. The rain has ceased, but the creek yet swells. And swiftly. Look!"

Maria did not answer. Neither did she turn around. She stood staring at the swirling water. Fence posts came down, broken planks, dead chickens, willow branches and brush-pine tips. Then a drowned goat which lodged against the bridge piling. Maria waded down to it, and remained.

"Señora! What do you see? . . . Doña Maria! It is dead!"

"Of course, fool!" she replied, coming back, wet to the waist. "But I saw on it the burnt three bars of Filadelfio Eluria. He lives up the steep cañon beyond Los Alamitos. . . . Burro! Are you yet blind to its meaning? How do you suppose this goat came here? There has been a cloudburst on the pine ridge between the high cañons of Luna and Lujan. The first rise of the river is coming. Get the people to the village. Sound the church bells. God knows what to expect."

The people fled on—save Maria, Teodosio and two other men. "For why?" chattered Teodosio. "Why do we remain? Look! Mother of God! What fury! In ten minutes the water will be over the bridge."

"It will be enough!" answered Maria curtly. "I have business across the bridge. Are you unaware that that is Don Fulgencio's old mill?"

One of the men stepped up. "Doña Maria. A thousand pardons. I am not unaware that he is your husband in name, and that you feel a certain anxiety about him now that the old blind crone, his sister, is dead. But look. The flood will sweep round the cliffs directly upon the mill. Not only that but the bridge will go out. Besides, he is probably not there."

"He is a fool, and you. Look!" She pointed across the river. Below the mill and under a great chestnut tree stood a tiny old man waving a stick. "Will one fool listen to another? I must talk to him myself." Maria shook off his arm and hurried across the bridge.

Above the roar of the water, as she approached, she could hear Fulgencio's screams. His sombrero had fallen off. His thin white hair stuck to his bony head like wet silk. He was soaking. "Away, cursed woman, who has laid a spell upon me!" he screamed, dancing about with his uplifted stick. "I saw you. I saw all the people you brought to gaze at me. You sent them away to hide behind the bushes. You come alone. But I see you and them. Away!"

The great chestnut stood on a small rise. The acequia had burst, the empty sluices were filling; from the mill above, water was streaming down upon the tree. But around it Fulgencio had been heaping up a tiny barricade of mud.

Maria rushed upon him. "Fool! Will you be drowned with your gold? Here, give me that shovel! We shall carry it into the mill where the walls are strong."

The old man let out a shriek of rage. "She told you! That magpie with no eyes and a loose tongue. She guessed and told you!" With a stick be beat down her upraised arms. They fought, sliding in the mud. But it was the old man's insane strength which secured the shovel. With a mighty swipe meant to take off her head, he leapt forward. Maria slipped; her feet went forward, her head back. The blade of the shovel caught her a glancing blow on the jaw. Teeth flew out, blood spurted. Her cleft chin opened like another but vertical mouth. Maria dropped like a log.

But now the men came running across the bridge. The old man leapt for the lower branches of the tree, and scrambled up to perch shrieking above them.

"Blessed Mother!" shouted one of the men. "He would have killed her who would have saved him. But there is no time to lose. The water washes over the bridge. Come. Let us get her between us. She awakes. Jesus, the blood! It is a miracle that we waited not too long to save her."

Halfway to the village, Maria came to her senses. She was being pulled along between two men, her chin held together by a strip of torn rebozo. Teodosio, in front, kept turning around to throw handfuls of muddy water in her face. "Blood and mud! You look like a slaughtered pig. And yet you keep mumbling of the gold necessary to rebuild our house. Mother of God! That day will never come. The valley is ruined forever. It is the day of judgment."

They reached Santa Gertrudes. The stub streets were filling with refugees from all directions, even from the pine slopes above. Among them milled horses, burros, cows, pigs and goats. The plaza in front of the church was packed solid with people. From the tower above, the bells were ringing. On the steps stood a priest, praying. Inside, a hasty mass was being said.

Suddenly the priest stopped his prayer. The bells stopped. In the tower a man had begun to shout. The first rise was coming down.

A cloudburst had broken in the high mountains to the north. Down the V-shaped cañons of Luna and Luján the water rushed to an apex, grew into a flood, and swept down the one narrow steep-walled cañon into the upper end of the valley.

Here, from the high Sangre de Cristo on the west, it was joined by the swollen Rio de la Casa. A mile farther, the flood separated to follow down the river to the east and the creek to the west, and thus spread into the already soaked valley from both sides.

As the water crept up to the village streets, Maria roused from her lethargy. She plucked Teodosio's sleeve, spit blood and another tooth. "These bells! This praying!" she said faintly. "I myself would trust high land to religion. Hoist me upon a loose burro. Let us go."

Again they plodded on. Up the steep little pass between

the valley and Ledoux. Others followed. A long bedraggled
line returning to the highlands whence they had come, if only
to prove that while misfortune seeks company, danger calls
them back to solitude. Here on the pine slope they looked
down to see the second rise sweep down the valley.

Two hours later a strange thing happened on the opposite
side. Just beyond the high cliffs at the curve of the crescent
valley a white snake leaped forth. It was transparent. In it
straws twisted and jammed and poked through the skin. The
snake roared and flashed. It tore loose great boulders as it
unrolled down the mountainside. Maria's apple trees lay
down before it. Swiftly it uncoiled, stretched and dived into
the creek. But still, unending, its body kept unrolling from
behind the cliffs.

Maria discovered her voice. "It is as I feared! As I said, yet
not as I said! It is worse! The flood comes down La Cañada
also!"

The cloudburst had broken in the high mountains to the
north drained by the Luna and Lujan which in turn empty
into the valley from the northwest. But between these cañons
and that of Guadalupita there is only a ridge of pines. The
clouds had but shifted slightly. And now the water coming
down La Cañada del Carro was sweeping into the valley from
the northeast. Into mid-valley, at the center of its crescent
beyond the jutting cliffs.

Maria saw her apple orchard sink, her barn float off in
pieces, her house become an island. And now, six feet high,
the snake rushed at Don Fulgencio's mill. The hewn stones
held—a small gray pillar in a surging flood. Surprisingly, the
old chestnut on its rise still stood, but half submerged in
water. And now through the afternoon the clumps of people
watched the water creep up into the village, a foot deep.

At dusk Teodosio found something to say. "They are
having a wet mass down there in the church. . . . But Jesus! It
cannot be so cold. . . . I shall try to light a fire. Did you bring
matches? I have none. Not in that pocket, nor in this. . . . "

At dawn they crept down the mountainside, halfstarved and stiff with cold. The water was receding, the sun coming out. It was unbelievable. It was ugly. It was revealing only an earth that was for them stricken and homeless, an earth that stank.

Bodies were being brought in, and reports of others. "Emeliano saw something sticking in the willows. . . . Myself and Abrán buried him, Señora. The head, you will realize . . . . It is best to be truthful in misfortune, Señora. . . . He will not return. My sympathy, Señora. . . . There where the crows and buzzards are already gathering. But yet the water is too high. Patience! And prayer!"

Maria listened. That night she heard of Don Fulgencio. His body had been found nearly a kilómetro downstream. He evidently had been swept from or fallen from the tree. "But the chestnut?" she asked. It still stood, but weakly, gouged out to its roots.

Maria sighed. Her sigh included, perhaps primarily, the lost box of gold pieces he had buried at the foot of the tree. Now there would be no money to rebuild and plant again.

In the morning she gathered together Niña and her daughter, Gertrudes and Teodosio. "Let us go back," she said stiffly, toothlessly.

"To what?" grumbled Teodosio. "Out of this you have a scar. A fine scar; nobody will recognize you. But nothing else. Mother of God! Not even a tooth! To say nothing of a place to sleep, a scrap of tortilla, a sip of water. Jesus! And I! I do not even have a cigarette. Not even a wet one. I tell you this has been a flood. Without doubt, a flood. Why. . . . "

7

At the age of seventy Maria was living alone in a small mountainside hut. It was the old one that lay in the little clearing just below the tall weathered cliffs which jut out to separate the crescent halves of the beautiful blue valley, and just above a steep corn milpa sloping up from the rutty cañon road. Thus unseeing eyes placed it. Maria, whose eyes saw it in time as well as in space, saw it as the point of a completed circle.

But Maria was a character. Such is regarded one who has outlived virtue and vice, having proved invulnerable to both and more powerful than either.

"She is strange and wise," people said of her.

The strangeness implied her uniqueness among their orthodoxy. The wisdom reflected her ability to see through their opinions.

"But I do not trust her fully," added some in a whisper.

Such a secret lack of faith do people below have in the truth that awaits above them.

Maria was content to wait. Seldom she allowed Teodosio

to drive her down into the valley in his rattletrap buggy. She only saw to it that he came up often enough to weed the corn and to bring her salt, sugar and tobacco. What more was necessary? She milked her goats, split her own wood; was too toothless to eat meat, too contented to require conversation, too busy to relish interruptions. "Besides," she said, "I can watch from here the empty doings of you all."

So she thrived on loneliness, and proved that energy creates inert mass. This energy, this understood vitality in one so old and wrinkled, she had sucked from her loves and labors, anxieties and follies, the illusions of her life. Its inert mass sat hour after hour, day by day, on top of the cliffs.

Below her the valley grew, new houses rose from the earth. New roads crawled up the cañons where only foot trails had come down. Burros diminished, rattling tin automobiles appeared—to be pulled out of chuck holes by teams and wagons, the mean that held between these extremes of travel. She saw the valley green, yellow and whiten, the mountain peaks step forth and back again into mists, scant harvests and days of plenty. Gringo voices came back, greaseless wagon hubs squeaked on frosty mornings, the church bells tolled births and deaths.

It all went on outside her as it went on in memory inside, changing but changeless, and thus an illusion. What remained was their common core. It was the reality she pondered.

Wind and rain matted her straggly hair. Sun and frost made leather of her swart cheeks and cleft chin. Her black, bright little eyes took on a queer remoteness. At times her steady gaze seemed turned inward—as if it had rounded the earth only to return to the duplicate within her.

But occasionally her meditations were interrupted. She had gone long to the people of the valley; now they came to her.

"Doña Maria," a man would say, respectfully standing before her, hat in hand, "you will forgive this interruption, but something is wrong with my house. It is a new house. It is a well built house. I built it with these hands. Yet something is wrong. In it I have always a cold, my wife sniffles, the noses of my children drip. It was not like this in our old house, which is now a stable—where no doubt our beasts are better off than we with colds."

"This new house of yours. It has windows?"

"Of glass, Señora! And two doors."

"It breathes through the eaves?"

"An air space, as they say. It is the new way."

"Pues!" grunted Maria. "These new ways! These new windows of glass by which one would be outside and in, at once! That is your trouble. Hereafter take care to stuff the eaves and doors. Remember this:

"When a draft gets at you through a hole,
Go make your will, and pray for your soul."

Advice on all matters she gave, and new remedies for old ills. Especially she recommended for headaches pieces of blue paper or the blue government tax stamps taken off tobacco cans and pasted on the forehead and around the eyes.

So her power still grew, and her name. She was not only a character but an institution. The trail up through the steep corn and pines to it wore deeper.

The fat, red-cheeked priest from the village church took it yearly. He came up hopefully, went down discouraged. "Father in Heaven! Give me strength! This miserable and faithless old woman is more powerful than a priest! Her fees are surely fatter!" Once he nearly swore.

It had happened on his autumnal visit to convert her to the faith, and so draw her power over the simple into the church, that he encountered her below the cliffs. She had driven down to her old home and orchard where Niña's family lived, Teodosio having moved with Gertrudes up the cañon. It had been a good apple year; there was a huge stack against the barn; Maria was in a tender humor.

"Let us have no empty words, Padre," she said kindly. "For twenty and more years I have heard your pleas, threats and arguments. They are all the same. I will listen no more. But of this heap of apples take plenty. Verdad! Fill your buggy. Take them to your church—wherever you will."

Niña's eyes popped. Teodosio's jaw dropped. But over the priest's red face crept a look of beatific triumph shadowed by a tiny irreconcilable doubt. Hastily, still smiling, he dropped to his knees, clasped his hands.

"God, O Father and His Blessed Son!" he prayed rapidly, before Maria could change her mind. "You have rewarded Your servant's toil of twenty years and more. To me it is to be given the baptising of this woman so long without faith and divine aid. Nor in my ecclesiastical joy am I unaware of those in this same church who preceded me in prayer for this admirable soul who gives this day in the name of the Father, the Son and Holy Ghost . . . ."

"Momentito, Padre!" interrupted Maria harshly. "What is all this about? I said merely to take apples to your church. The pigs will eat no more."

The story spread. Men in the cantinas roared, women tittered in the stores; the whole valley shook with laughter. The remark became a saying. "Take it! The pigs will eat no more!" Thus they joked when giving the unneeded to one another.

The priest's visit was followed by Pierre Fortier's. He was no longer merely a shopkeeper who sold clothes and canned goods, fresh meat, harness and tiny sewing machines; who bought wool, hides and grain by the car load. He was something of an art dealer. Agents from the cities came to him for arrowheads, for old tinwork, leather trunks and great carved chests, for precious old blankets and lacework, and for Santos of all kinds—the carved bultos and the retablos or tablas painted on wood or tin.

Old Pierre had a nose for all these things. He had lived in the valley a lifetime. Every hut in all its cañons he knew, and

if it contained an unknown treasure: an old carven chest
from Mexico half sunk in the damp earth floor, a browned
old Santo hanging above the rickety bed. Moreover he knew
the idiosyncrasies of their owners.

"This dirty old chest!" he would say, giving it a kick. "The
wood is rotting away! Bring it in some day when I am in a
good humor. Perhaps I can find use for it as a wood box, and
give your wife a new dress on credit. In such a tidy house it is
a disgrace. But not today, compadre!"

Those places where the Santos were stubbornly clung to
by the old, he merely noted. This old woman would die soon;
her son liked whiskey.

What he had long wanted from Maria was an old
burnt-orange Chimayó blanket. One edge was tattered, it had
holes. It was dirty, it was thin. But whenever Pierre saw it
glowing in the sunlight, felt its weave and wonderful softness,
his mouth watered. "Mon Dieu! It is a blanket too good for
the top of a piano in a home of the rich. It is fit for a
museum. An old woman who yet knows the old way, to
patch the holes. Another to wash it in amole. Yes. Then for
this blanket I could begin to ask seven hundred dollars!"

But also every time he saw it he groaned. Maria used it in
Teodosio's buggy. When the blanket was thrown over the seat
the protruding springs poked through the weave. When it lay
over her lap she trod most of it underfoot. Always it was
assaulted by the sun and dust, by rain and hail and snow.
And Teodosio used it to cover his horses.

Where this old blanket came from Maria did not remember. She had never been without it, even as a child. So she
ignored first the gruff and then the polite preludes of Pierre
to buy it.

On the day he came up to Maria's hut, Teodosio's old
buggy was waiting at the foot of the trail. In its seat lay the
blanket. Pierre's eyes gleamed. He rubbed his long black
whiskers, and on his wooden leg stamped wheezing up the
slope. Maria he hugged and kissed on both cheeks.

"By Jesus, old friend! I tramp up this cursed steep trail to commiserate with another old and poor, broken in health and miserable. To find you sound as mountain beef, glowing with health and bubbling joy through bright eyes! Are you in love, have you found the fountain of youth? For shame, having not told me, your oldest friend. Why do you never come down to see me?"

To Teodosio he even gave a cigarette.

His visit was brief; he was buying cattle, he said. And when Teodosio left, Pierre accompanied him down the trail. At their adjacent buggies he stopped. As if on a sudden impulse, he jerked out of his own a new, bright-colored Navajo blanket, and spread it carefully over Teodosio's seat.

"We have been compadres for uncounted years," he said, slapping Teodosio on the back. "As a present I give you this fine new blanket. May comfort and protection, pleasure and joy, it give you both. . . . But I shall just take away this forlorn old rag that you have been forced to use all these years. . . . Adiós, compadre!"

When a few days later Maria asked for her old blanket, she was presented with the new one. She inspected it silently, its color, its weave and design. She drove down to Pierre's store with Teodosio.

Pierre was out in the mountains. She sat down on a sack of pintos. She waited all morning. She waited half the afternoon.

"What is it, Señora? Is it important, as surely it must be, that which keeps you waiting?"

"Well, it is about that faded old red blanket that Señor Fortier took of me. . . . I forgot to tell him that it was full of bugs. Bugs of sickness." Maria fixed the clerk with a shrewd look. I can trust you? Maria can trust a boy who seems so bright and helpful, who will keep his counsel? . . . Well then, listen. Those bugs of sickness were none other than the plague itself! Now! Do you see my anxiety, its importance? I shudder to think of the hands—whose hands, amiguito, have touched it?"

"But three, Doña Maria.—Thank God, not mine!—Those of Señor Fortier himself. Those of the old woman whom he gave it to mend, those of her who washes it now."

"Excellent! To them I shall go at once with herbs to relieve them of possible danger. Their names quickly! And to Señor Fortier when he returns, my thanks for his gift."

Maria obtained her blanket from her who had washed it. "Pierre Fortier will pay as agreed. Give him my thanks for washing it, amiga. It has never been so clean and soft."

To the woman who had mended it she went with a message. "Pierre Fortier will pay. But give him my thanks for mending it, amiga. It is as good as new."

Maria rode home content. It was an old blanket, though mended and washed; it was true it had once covered a child with the plague. Yet she liked it, and thenceforth slept under it.

Behind her she left Pierre Fortier cursing in French and stamping his wooden leg. Throughout the village and echoed up the cañons shouted the gossip. "My thanks, compadre. But Pierre Fortier will pay."

"Mother of God!" people laughed. "What a strange and wise old woman! She fears neither God nor man. She has a mind of her own, has Doña Maria. It knows everything."

It is true that those who laughed the loudest feared worst the priest and owed Pierre Fortier the most. It is the tribute of slaves to bondage, that they never learn to use their strength in freeing themselves, but only to applaud others.

Maria sitting in silence on her crags neither heard nor needed their approbation. It was sunset. The valley before her deepened in color from plum to blue; it was no less beautiful when blue-black. Behind her in the little clearing among the pines waited her little hut—no larger, no more changed than it had been, off and on when patched, for seventy years. It was the point of her completed circle. She too had endured unchanged.

She had withstood the ebb and flow of the seasons; the sullen hostility of commerce and misfortune; the anaesthesia of religion, wealth and acclaim—all the passions that warp the mind, flesh and spirit of man.

She was immune from all but the ultimate destruction of her inessential outer shell.

At eighty, she heard of the dam.

It is late afternoon. The whole day in the valley has churned like a fiesta. Wagons loaded with people rumble down the cañons. Double-mounted horses too have passed: the front rider with left foot in the stirrup and leaning sideways, the rider behind him with right foot in the stirrup and leaning to the opposite side,—the old way, when mounts are scarce and must carry double over the rocky trails. Men have left their fields, women their houses and wood piles. The roads are full. Santa Gertrudes and San Antonio both swarm. From each, continually, a battered tin automobile chugs up one cañon after another and returns with a load of people.

It is not a Día de Fiesta. It is not a Saint's Day to be celebrated. It is Election Day in the beautiful blue valley.

Across from the courthouse in Santa Gertrudes stands a gaunt adobe. It is unfurnished save for a wooden platform at one end. Here each Saturday night, and all day during fiesta, sit the guitar players who pluck out music for dances. Today the floor is even more crowded. The walls are lined with tables partially screened by mosquito netting. Near the door sits a man at a table with two huge boxes. It is the place of voting.

The road in front is crowded. The sheriff and two deputies wear their guns outside their coats. The deputies are too drunk to use them. The sheriff cannot read the sign which says in English that no electioneering is permitted here.

When the crowded Ford sputters up and unloads, he makes way for driver and passengers and a político who meets them. The político smokes a cigar and wears a cloth vest.

"Ah, you brought them," he says to the driver. "Our good friends from up the cañon! Welcome. Welcome, amigos."

The passengers have no shoes. They are rudely dressed in dirty gingham and black rebozos, in denims and leather vests. Their eyes shine like polished obsidian.

"To you our devout thanks. We have never ridden in a máquina before. Our wits are turned by its swiftness. We were there and then here. A day's hard journey transformed into the flight of an hour. It is a miracle!" she stoops and kisses the político's hand.

"Por nada, por nada!" he answers gruffly. "Here are your papers."

They look at the sample ballots wonderingly. None can read.

"What is the name of him for whom we mark the cross this time, Señor? Is it a new Gobierno? Perhaps a new Presidente, himself? Strange. We have had no pictures of him for our windows. We have heard no talk."

"Bastante, compadre! It is not a great man you vote for this day, but a great thing. Your hand is put to the paper so that there will be no more floods to sweep cañon and valley with death and destruction, that there will be water for all in time of drought, that it will be measured, to each his proper share. The Government can do all this. But it wishes the sign of your will. . . . Here now! Each! See, I have marked on your paper the tiny crosses. Inside, Fidencio will give you others like this, but empty. Fill them with crosses as these, without mistake. Thus you will do your duty!"

Slowly the people file inside. Carefully, tenderly, they spread out the clean sheets on the little tables, lest they be soiled. Pencil stubs they lick with nervous lips, and hold awkwardly in calloused brown hands. They talk through the mosquito netting. "See? I have made the crosses as instructed. Do they look right to you, primo? I would not have the Government consider me too ignorant though I cannot read."

At the center table they give their ballots to Fidencio. He looks them over casually, and stuffs them in a box.

Outside, the político gives each man a sack of tobacco and each woman a stick of candy. They are hurriedly stuffed back into the car.

"Have you got them all?" the político asks the driver in English. "Know anybody else? Anybody, anywhere! If they won't come get their names. Get the names of their horses, their cows and pigs and dogs. Where is that list of names you brought from the graveyard? We might need that too.... Now get on! For God's sake! Give her another twist."

And til dark the battered tin máquina chugs back and forth from the dark cañons.

Maria has watched it steadily, all day, from the top of her cliffs. She rises stiffly and walks down to her hut. In the dusky clearing she chops a few sticks. She boils tea, spoons some beans with pieces of a torn tortilla, puts up the tea leaves to use again with fresh.

It is eight thousand feet high, and already cold. Her mind is cold with foreboding, too. She huddles before the blaze without moving. An hour. Two. Her thoughts begin to boil. Her old, dark and impassive face thaws into wrinkles. Her loose lips draw back from her one tooth. Suddenly, savagely, she spits into the coals.

"Los Mofres! Those cursed Mofres!"

Many, many years ago when Maria was a goat girl, a stranger had wandered into the beautiful blue valley. He had blue eyes, fair skin and a sharp tongue which lurked behind a perpetual smile. On his broad back he wore a pack. His hands were clever at mending broken pots, and dexterous at warding off occasional knife thrusts with the staff he carried. He was an itinerant peddler, an Irishman from County Donegal, and his name was Thomas Murphy.

Respect gathered round him with the walls of the beautiful valley. Perhaps its own blue seemed green. He remained. Soon his brother came, bringing a wife for each. Shortly they had land at the mouth of one of the little cañons. And before long, Tomás had a house and a store, and Roberto a house and a tiny mill for grinding the grain both raised and which Tomás sold.

It was amazing how they prospered. Their land grew and was fruitful. The store enlarged, rivaled Pierre Fortier's. The little water mill duly supplanted the big one of the Garcias. Sons and daughters came in abundance, grandchildren. Finally, with all of these, came power.

The source of this power really lay in a hairline difference between them and the people of the valley. Outwardly they lived as all. Their Spanish was even better. The women could dish up costillas adobadas flavored to the exact heat with chile carribe and dance a varsoviana as gracefully as any neighbor. The men could rope and tie a wild steer as quick, and hold as much liquor. To their own innumerable Celtic superstitions they added those of the valley. Their first born sons they sent to the priest as altar boys for training. And by most they were accepted not as the only gringos to remain in the valley, but as proper vecinos. Their name was changed from "Murphy" to the more easily pronounced "Mofre," and the little cañon they controlled became known as "El Cañon de Mofre."

But inwardly they remained gringos and Irish. As gringos they held to a certain cold objectivity which enabled them to see themselves apart from the land and the people. As Irishmen they felt it incumbent to always get a shade the better of both. In trade, land and argument, they were still sharp peddlers.

The one trait they inherently possessed in common with their neighbors was a natural gravitation toward politics. Drunken rows, cold scheming and hot arguments over candidates for a school teacher, a county clerk, a new sheriff—these offered a pleasure surpassing that in a good trade. They became politicos.

Los Mofres then, through land, business and politics,

became a power in the beautiful blue valley.

Maria did not trust them. year by year she watched them fence in a piece of land, a field here, a few varas there, and still another pasture. Year by year she heard of another paisano falling into debt to store or mill. She began to smell a rat.

There is the power of the mind. It says, "There are no tribes, no races, no peoples separated by the color of their eyes, their hair and skin. There is only mankind. All men are brothers. Each has the same passions, thirsts and hungers. The greed for gold and the greed for land is common to all. The Murphys of the world have it, as do I. I will not unjustly condemn my brother."

But there is also the power of the blood which keeps beating, "There are many earths, and each has its own irreconcilable spirit of place. Now what is a man but his earth? It rises in walls to shelter him in life. It sinks to receive him at death. By eating its corn he builds his flesh into walls of this selfsame earth. He has its granitic hardness or is soft resiliency. He is different as each field even is different. Thus do I know my own earth; I can know no other. I am greedy for my land, and that is right. Does not a child cry for its mother's breasts? But when the Murphys desire my land, it is false. For they would not belong to it; they would only that it belonged to them. By this they refute their own mother, and would enslave another's for a ransom of gold. So I suspect them."

Maria listened, and remained silent. But watchful.

Into the valley came talk of a dam. There came strange gringos who answered to no names as men standing on their own feet, but whose mother was the same, "La Compañía de Agua y Tierra de Demora." With the Mofres they talked. Always.

A little longer, and the Mofres supplied beef and mutton for a fiesta down in the campo below the village. Many important men, they said, would be there to tell the good people of the valley, our neighbors, about the dam. The dam of which you have heard, no doubt. Has there not been talk?

So all the good people of the valley assembled on the campo. Maria went herself. And there were the important men who talked about the dam to all, men of the Government, of the State, the nameless men of the Company, officials, políticos. And beside them, looking more important than all, the Mofres.

Instantly, intuitively, Maria distrusted the dam. She rode home perplexed. She withheld judgment. But all the time she pondered the question up and down, back and forth.

The dam had its virtues, no doubt. There had always been floods, down one cañon, then another, and once from two—Madre mia! There had always been droughts which were equally bad. Now with a dam, as it was said, there would be no floods and no droughts bearing death and destruction in each. There would be water at all times, measured to each man his proper share.

But this dam is to be built only for the benefit of the good people of the valley, and the Mofres' eagerness for it, did not quite coincide in Maria's mind.

The Mofres loved the good people of the valley, their neighbors. They loved them, besought them with great credit in store and mill. "Just sign this paper, compadre, to show that it is not your will to forget." And then, very quickly, they took away their land for payment.

Mother of God! Can one believe a man who says he loves his family, when he allows one member to starve? Can a man love his country, and yet neglect his own field?

There is no patriotism beyond the few leagues we would really die for. There is no love of abstract humanity. There is only the love we show each man as an individual.

So Maria questioned the Mofres' intent to benefit the people by the dam while they robbed them individually. She wondered what they would derive from a dam that would control the cañon water for their mill instead of themselves.

She wondered how they would exact payment for the beef and mutton eaten at the fiesta.

The election came. People waited to hear Maria's opinion. Some went to her. She was silent. So they listened to the busy Mofres and to the políticos who sputtered up the cañons, they accepted rides in the máquina to mark their crosses as instructed, candy and tobacco. The políticos came up for Maria.

"Just what is this election?" she asked quietly.

"Well," answered one man, with the ready formula. "It is for the people to express their will for a dam. That there may be no more floods, no more droughts, but water always, as needed. Is it not a wonderful thing?"

Said another who knew Maria's shrewdness, "Madre, it is the water district election, granted by our county commissioners whom we elected ourselves."

Maria rolled a cigarette. "Water District?" she asked slowly. "Is there not water in all districts?"

"It is like this, Madre. Allow me to explain fully. This valley is one water district of many in these parts. It is a judicial district. It is a County. Do you see? When one regards water, it is as a water district. When one regards justice and law, it is as a judicial district. When one regards government, it is as a County. And none of these districts, of which there are many of each, may be different and thus interfere with the others. Thus we are the United States! Now do you understand? We are no longer merely the valley."

"No, amigo," said Maria puffing deliberately. "It is you who are dumfounded with words. We are still the valley. Water is our problem; our fights over a stream's flow have always been the fiercest; too much of it has killed us also. We have out Masters of the Ditch. Hence also our need for justice, for government. But with all of these, and more, Señor, we are still the valley. The mountains enclose us, the earth feeds us. It is a thing of itself. Do not talk of a district on paper!

"But how—granting what you say—will this dam be built if it is the will of the people? Who will pay? We ourselves are too poor."

The político alternated between impatience to be off and the desire to show his great knowledge of these matters.

"Señora," he stated tersely. "You will not understand, nor is there reason to. The election for the dam will win. Its results will be an issue of papers worth money—bonds, the great men call them. These will be sold in the city by the officiales. This money will pay for half the dam. It will be given to the Government which will then supply the other half, and build the dam. The Government, Señora. For the people. For water conservation and safety."

"And what will the people in the city do with the paper they have bought? I cannot imagine . . . . "

"It is clear, Doña Maria, that you have no mind for such matters, despite being the widow of Señor Garcia whose knowledge of these things—and money—was profound. He himself was of this Demora Water and Land Company, as are the Mofres—two of them. Besides being, one of them, a Water Commissioner. . . . I may add, however, that this illustrious Company will no doubt buy much of that paper. They will then collect money from the people they save from death and destruction. In taxes. So much for the water they use. No more than reasonable, of a certainty. Are they not our neighbors? . . . Bastante! We must be off. No one else has asked so many questions. . . . Come now, Doña Maria. We will help you mark your paper with a cross for this great thing."

"I shall not vote," replied Maria wearily. "As you see, I am old and weak. That swift máquina would break all my brittle bones. . . . Go with God, Señores—you do not have far to go."

For two days she sat alone, studying this new problem. She had the miraculous memory of those who do not read and write. Moreover her years with Don Fulgencio had already opened to her the new world of worldly matters. She was more shrewd than anyone—even Don Fulgencio—had suspected.

On the third day she had Teodosio drive her down to the village. The overwhelming results of the election had just been announced. She also nursed the new fact that Don Fulgencio had been a member of this water and land company. She went to the courthouse, puffed up the warped pine steps to the office of the recorder. He was an old man, this Sanchez, with puffed cheeks and small eyes. He had been a friend of Don Fulgencio.

For twenty minutes they battled with elaborate politeness.

"To the point!" directed Maria sharply. "I come in haste and in distress. I am old. I shall soon be dead. How much land do I own? Get out the papers. . . . We are going to have a dam. Advise me, as a trusted friend of your friend, my husband, about this dam and my land."

Sanchez tottered over his maps as if he did not know that she knew every tree, rock and ravine that marked the limits of her land.

"Your strip of land here, from the tall cliffs across the valley to the opposite mountains. . . . This piece, your share from one Onesimo. . . . These pieces of your children, Refugio Montes, Gertrudes Paiz and Antonio de la Vega, yet in your name, as that of Teodosio and Niña. All in the valley, Señora. That without, you have already sold."

Maria brushed back her thin gray hair. "Sold? Yes, of course. But my memory fails. What land did you say, amigo?"

Sanchez blinked his small eyes suspiciously. Maria drew out from her tattered rebozo a heavy, yellow coin. It was square in shape, and gold. Her old wrinkled hands turned it idly as she watched the greedy glitter come into his eyes. Then she slid the gold piece across the table. He clutched it; it was gone.

"Come, Sanchez!" Her voice was hard, metallic. "All what land? My memory weakens. Refresh it, Sanchez."

"Why surely you remember! All that land up in the mountains. Beyond the valley. The share which was yours equally with that in the valley, according to the old Grant," he went on complacently. "The original Spanish land grant to the first seventy-six settlers in the valley. It gave them not only the land within the valley which they developed and was all they could use or want. It gave them all the land outside, nearly the whole Condado, which they forgot.

"Now the time came when this grant was confirmed by the new gringo government. And the time came, as you remember, when all the descendants of these seventy-six were given titles to their land, and the Presidente caused these titles to be made Patent. Now a title to every piece of land within the valley was also a title to a share without—ten times the size. But who remembered? Nobody. Save Don Fulgencio, Señora.

"Cómo no? He was simply shrewd and careful. It was business. Like this. A poor farmer comes to him for a loan on his land, with land to sell. My wise friend takes title to all his land—the piece within the valley the man knows he owns, and the larger piece outside that he knows nothing about. Pretty soon the man raises a little money, he wants his land back—it is the Devil the way they hang on to their land! So my friend simply transfers back to him his valley land, and retains title to the rest. No one is the wiser."

"Ah!" sighed Maria.

"Ah, indeed! What a head he had on those narrow shoulders of his, Don Fulgencio, my friend, your husband! Most of this land was mountainous, fit only for grazing. But he smelled the new railroad approaching, which needed timber for ties. . . . But more important! This land was on the watershed. With it water rights could be controlled when eventually a dam was needed. There was even a Compañía forming. And Don Fulgencio had the land. So he became one with the Compañía. Only one piece more was needed. You remember? Title to that long cañon draining into the valley past the tall cliffs. The perfect site for a dam that must be built.

"My memory returns, Sanchez," said Maria soberly.

"As I thought!" he replied shrewdly. "A great price Don Fulgencio must have got for it, too, from the Compañía. Why, for ten years I myself watched pass the timber they cut from it to sell the railroad. To say nothing of all the other land like it he got from these dull people, our neighbors. I myself arranged the papers of title for him—at very little profit to myself, for keeping a tongue in my cheek. Though he promised more. But died too soon." He was eyeing Maria steadily now. "Of course you are poor according to custom, Doña Maria. As was he, being wise. But a little of that gold now. . . ."

Maria stood up. "Enough! Well do I recognize my husband's shrewdness in being a político to maintain you in office. You who are so cunning yourself. But I think not too poorly paid for what you have done. No doubt these new políticos, the Mofres, who have taken up the dead one's power, pay you less than he. Verdad?"

"A little but not enough. Cristo Rey! But when the dam is built, and they have the water to measure and sell, and theirs is the new electric plant, and taxes moreover—well, it is best to bet on the winning horse. . . . But now. About this land of yours. That in the valley. The piece by the tall cliffs. It is good with respect to the dam. Very good, I will say to you with the memory of Don Fulgencio between us. But, as you say, you are getting old. If you would sell, to the Mofres I myself . . . ."

"No, amigo. No, my cunning friend. I have decided not to sell my land. Not a vara. Now I must go. To you I leave the memory of Don Fulgencio and a piece of his gold. I would not know what to do with either."

Sanchez looked at her curiously as she went out.

Winter crept down the mountains. The valley paled from a lake of blue to a lake of white. Cold clutched and throttled it. And then its white turned blue again with the shadowy reflection of the peaks upon its icy crust.

So do men, their deeds blanketed, still reflect the natural color of their lives.

Maria from her cliffs watched the mutations. She knew at last why Don Fulgencio had desired her in marriage. But so long ago! It meant nothing to her now. He was but one of many, his shape a shadow mirrored for an instant upon the one enduring earth.

For days, a week, she was snowbound. It gave her time to properly consider the dam. There was this about it, it was more than a dam, it was a step in progress. And progress men define as that step toward giving the greatest good to the greatest number of people. Now Maria believed neither in the majority nor in the minority. She believed in all men. Good for the strong at the expense of the weak she saw as a natural inevitability. But also she saw that intentional wrong dealt the few can never be paid for by the right derived from it by the many. Maria believed in fulfillment instead of progress. Fulfillment is individual evolution. It requires time and patience. Progress, in haste to move mass, admits neither.

So she pondered, beating her way up the snowy trail to her seat on the crags, and wrapping herself in the soft burnt-orange blanket.

The suspicion never entered her head that she was philosophizing. She thought that she was making up her mind about the dam. It merely shows how abstract are all things in perspective when seen from a height. In dimensional time and space nothing is only what it seems.

Over the icy fields below her raced a spot of black. It had length and breadth, form and movement. Yet deep ravines did not halt it, nor rocky slopes, nor fences. It was the shadow of a crow in swift flight overhead.

The dam too would cast a shadow. The misfortune of men who would lose their land would not stop it. It would flit across their lives with fear and suffering, anger and evil. All shadows of the shadow of the dam itself. But can you tell a man who starves that his hunger is unreal? Can you tell a man that his own life is but a shadow when he has no eyes to see the real?

Maria sighed. How long it had taken her to climb above it all, this valley of illusion with its pain and incomprehension! Yet to it she was still bound. There is no philosophy of value which would deny the earth below. For it is life with its injustice and cruelty, and its patience to suffer both, which gives us even the philosophy to lift ourselves above it.

The wind had come up again. It curled round the crags streamers of snow. It shrieked through the pines, whistled over the rocks. The leaden skies dropped and crushed its voice and action. The pandemonium became a pause.

Maria trudged back to her hut. Another snow was coming. She would need plenty of wood.

The snow came, a foot of it and more. Another came, and yet another. A day of sun welded the layers together. The earth became solid as a frozen peach. And still the cold persisted. Twice a night she got up stiffly to replenish the fire. For water she had to chop up the stream. The pine outside split open with cold. In the clearing, gaunt, heavy-headed deer stood up to their bellies in snow. With them Maria shared her own corn.

Late in February winter broke. The earth began to soften like a spoiled peach. Its muddy juice ran down cañon and mountainside. The roads began to open. Soon came Teodosio. She could hear the squeak of his greaseless hubs a kilómetro away.

For an hour they sat talking in the hut. Then Maria got up and placed a bag of pesos in his hands.

"There are twenty pesos," she said sharply. "You will say there are not enough. But with them I want that old buggy fixed. A new tongue. Rims for three wheels. A bit of leather. Much grease. Perhaps a lantern to tie behind. No less! The last time I rode, the wheel broke; I would not fall again."

"Mother of God! Such expense. To say nothing of the

work to me. Why, to fix it as you say would require a
fortune. Do you think it has remained the same? Jesus,
Madre! Now the top is gone. The seat is hard with chicken
droppings. Its. . . ."

"Enough! Let it be fixed with your work and my pesos."

"For why? By all the Saints. . . . "

"Because," answered Maria slowly, "because I have remained up here alone too long. Spring comes. We ride down
through the valley as before. There are things that need my
attention. Especially this new dam. I do not approve of it."

8

The first cocks were crowing into the darkness when a faint, low chanting murmured across the fields. Unhurried and throaty with sleep, it moved slowly up the valley growing in volume but not in tempo. Under this polyphony beat another rhythm, an undertone of shuffling feet and the muffled allegro of still more running from out of the scattered adobes on each side. It was a centipedal procession of voice and feet.

Near the bottom of the jutting cliffs the lifting darkness revealed its body—a long column of shivering legs, thinly wrapped thick torsos and bare bent heads. The procession turned right and straggled up the curving cañon. A kilómetro and more up, it turned left out of the pallid gray road. The narrow trail wound up through a steep corn milpa freshly plowed, into pines, past a little hut in a clearing.

Voice and foot became louder now. Dislodged stones rattled down the mountainside from the more steeply rising trail. Breaths came shorter, hoarser. But still all sang, raising their eyes to stare upward and forward toward the looming crags.

At their head climbed four old men alternately carrying on two of their shoulders a statue of a fifth tottering on a little wooden platform. The latter was older than all four. His wooden cheeks were cracked, his painted skin peeling. Only his eyes were bright and timeless, little marbles of shiny agate. In one hand, for a staff, he held a wooden spade. At his feet stood a yoke of oxen no bigger than rabbits.

"Courage, San Ysidro!" panted one of the old men, respectfully, stopping to steady the statue with a hand almost as brown and lifeless. "It has been a long climb. But we are in time. Mira! The day is just breaking."

They reached the top of the tall cliffs. On the top-most crag sat an old wrinkled woman wrapped in a faded burnt-orange blanket. She did not turn around at sound of their chanting, nor to watch them group around the rocks below her. She pushed back her thin, flying hair, and continued staring fixedly down into the beautiful blue valley.

The sun was rising. Little javelins of sunlight struck the opposite wall of the mountains, were deflected back by cliff and rock, or fell split and broken down the water-gashed hillsides. The air grew luminous with spears and arrows of gold. Pine needles glistened metallically. Micaceous rocks glittered like cut diamonds. Streams flowed silver. Far off, a window glass gleamed crystal.

Then suddenly the mist lifted. Down below spread out the squares and rectangles and strips of black, fresh plowed earth—the fresh, deep, soft earth of spring.

"The Salida del Sol! Look, San Ysidro!" a deep voice cried out in the pause. "It is your day, el Día de San Ysidro Labrador, the blessed saint of farmers, the precious patron of our fields and crops. It is your day, and sunrise of that day. Now we have brought you to these high cliffs so that you may overlook all our fields and see that our fields are ready, our crops in. Bless them therefore, San Ysidro, on account of our devoutness, our readiness and labor, that they may this year bear fruitfully."

The deep, slow chant burst out afresh. The old men hoisted the little platform still higher, carried it to the edge of the cliffs, turned it slowly this way and that, all ways. And San Ysidro from his bright, shiny little eyes of agate stared down at Santa Gertrudes and San Antonio, at El Alto de Talco and El Alto de los Herreras, at all the little clumps of adobes in the long blue crescent, and saw that all the land between was black and fresh and ready.

"Lift him higher, Padre!" shouted a paisano pointing to a narrow cañon mouth. "My land is high. It is partly hidden by those pines. But I want him to see it is ready, for all those cursed stones that chipped my plow."

"Turn him this way! No, that!" demanded another crowding to the front of the crowd. "I would have him know that it is yet too early to plant my crop, being but the middle of May, yet see that my land is all prepared and ready for the seed. Gracias, Señores. Mil gracias."

Through all this singing, these exhortations, the old woman above did not stir. Nor did she turn around at silence when all knelt on the rocks in a prelude to prayer. She continued staring down into the sun-flooded valley.

The men rose from their knees. They flashed quick looks at her above them, and then plodded in noisy groups back down the trail. The Santo had done his duty as they. Now they were men hungry for porridge and tortillas, and he was a piece of wood. So they passed him cumbersomely from arm to arm, and unmindfully cracked the little wooden platform against protruding rocks. But the woman, having both the qualities of saint and man, they still respected. They did not speak until they had passed her hut.

Two old men remained on the cliffs. They approached the topmost crag.

"Well, Doña Maria," said one, respectfully enough. "It is the middle of May. It is el Día de San Ysidro Labrador. It is just past the rising of the sun. Now we have done as you suggested, according to the old custom. Did we not do it right? Did we not do it well? What do you think of it, Doña Maria?"

"And what do you think of the future of our crops?" added the other shrewdly. "Will we have a heavy harvest?"

Maria screwed around in her seat on the rocks, and focused on them her small bright eyes.

"Pues! How now do you feel about this thing, yourselves, compadres? Have you no feelings in those brittle bones that you must ask me for mine?"

The two old men stepped back. One of them began to study his feet. Said the other, "Well, I, Señora. . . . Well now I will say this. I feel very good about this thing. It is queer but so. I feel like the young man I was when I first climbed up here on San Ysidro's day. How many years has it made? Quien sabe? I know only that it was my first piece of land, the first wife I had to feed from it. Now the blessed Santo did not fail me that first year. He has not failed me since—only off and on, perhaps, for which any Santo can be duly excused, this being earth and not heaven. So I say, and truly it is my opinion, that it has not been a good thing to forget this old custom of late, and that it is a good thing to continue it again. . . . Madre! I had forgotten how beautiful the fresh black earth looks from here on high, in spring, with the crows busy already. . . . Not only I, Señora. I saw other eyes and in them the wonder. Did you ever see so many as came? At a suggestion. At a nod. So far too. So steep. . . . It makes me hungry for hot coffee. For an egg, perhaps. . . . "

Maria spat. "There are no eggs! There is no coffee! Am I rich that I can eat thus every morning? But in my house there are no doubt tortillas. And tea. I have used it but once. With a little fresh it will be black enough. And hot—if you cut a little wood."

She began to unbend, very stiffly and slowly. Then suddenly, one foot down, she spoke to the other old man. "Señor! You ask of the future of your crops. Pues! Tell all who so bade you ask, this: It will be a good year. The best in five. Is it enough? Now come. We shall have that tea. For two men who must depend on an old woman for their faith as well as their breakfast, you have not done badly with this procession."

When they had gone, Maria lay down underneath a pine for a morning nap. The stream beside her gushed full and noisy with melting snow from the peaks still white above. Even with little rain the acequias would be full all summer. She belched, then sighed with wisdom.

It is impossible to fight the new with its own weapons. But to go back, back to the dimly understood truths that lie dormant in dead faiths and living bloodstreams—that is the secret of seers and dictators, of power and success. For mechanical progress, being change, is evanescent. What endures is only the enduring.

So she began to fight the dam: not opposing it with any reason, but calling forth the feeling for the land it would supplant.

There was much time, for still the season paraded, and there was no dam.

"What is this?" a villager would ask. "Where is that dam for which we marked our crosses as directed so long ago? The Government has failed us."

And soon they almost forgot it.

But always, at dawn, noon or night, one might glimpse an old buggy stopped in the middle of a road. Over forty years old it was—that part of the original which still remained to squeak and groan and flap in the wind. Automobiles jolted past in whirls of dust which choked the old woman stiffly upright in the tattered seat. Bands of horsemen, groups of women, plodded by. But oblivious of them all, an old white-headed scarecrow of a man in a rusty suit stood at the side letting water.

"Sacred Heart of Jesus!" she would exclaim when he clambered up again. "Have you no control over your water?

It makes three times already that you have been out. And those pantalones! Have they no buttons?"

"Of course, of course," grumbled the old man. "But it is cold. How can I wait? Besides, my kidneys are shattered with all this traveling from dawn to dusk. Cristo!" He slapped the skeleton horses into a walk again. "Andelante! Nosotros no somos congrejos! We are not crabs!"

It was a specter, this rattletrap buggy drawn by a skeleton team, and containing an old white-headed man and a dark wrinkled witch—the specter of Maria fighting the specter of a dam.

Suddenly both assumed more reality.

The rich people in the city had finally bought those papers of the Compañía. The papers from which the dam would be built. Much money it required. Not a thousand pesos, Señor. Ten thousand! And more, though I cannot imagine more. It has all been given to the Government. Now the President will build the dam. He has not forgotten, after all. Imagine that, compadres!

The Mofres and the Compañía gave another fiesta. They shot off fireworks. These, beyond words, were beautiful. There were stars of hope, flowers of fire, flashing blades of passion, bright streamers of desire arching the heavens. And all in color. Such colors. Magnífico!

Old Tiburcio, he who was called "El Tigre," saw them from his hut in the mountains. He lashed his horse to town in a lather, and flung off to grovel on the church steps. He thought that the end of the world, by fire, had come.

"Courage, primo! Have no fear!" he was counseled, with many reassuring thumps on the back. "It is but these new fireworks you see for the first time. Hah! Great days are coming. You will see greater things yet no doubt when the Government comes to build this dam."

Maria continued to drive around in her buggy.

"A fine stand of oats you have," she would say to a man. "A beautiful piece of land. There is none better. Well, treasure it and find comfort in it while you may. Soon it will be nothing but a lake. You will have to make your living fishing, though in winter you will probably starve. You have voted to give up your land to this new dam."

To another with skin trouble she would recommend this remedy: tierra blanca and raw frijoles ground together. "Beans you may obtain from any man. But this tierra blanca found on your own ranchito is the best I know. As you know, half the walls in the valley are washed with it. Such a shame that you would give it up for this dam."

As she rode away each stared after her with a look of dull bewilderment.

But now the day was set; the day when all the people were to come to town for a big talk. Little posters appeared in store windows, on fenceposts, adobe walls and tacked upon great pines. Officers of the water district had called a meeting to ask landowners to agree upon a price for their land.

Maria set her jaw, ignored her rheumatism, and rode doggedly from house to house. This time she talked plainly. When a man saw her coming, he hastily summoned his neighbors. They gathered round her buggy with hats removed.

"Doña Maria, I have called my primos to listen also. We know you do not like this dam, but we have forgotten why. You will pardon our short memories, for you know that we are simple. Now tell us again what we should think."

Maria spat over the dashboard. "Are you men or are you children? Listen! You have heard that the dam is good. It is good because after it there will be no more floods, no more droughts, but water always for each man according to his need. Is not that what the políticos told you, los Mofres, the agents of the Compañía?"

"Verdad! Not a word has she left out. What a memory she has. . . . Sí, Sí, Señora. It is as they said."

"All right, Señores," said Maria patiently. "Let us say that this dam will do all these things. Now answer me this. Think well, amigos." On each simple face in turn she fixed her gaze. "Guadalupe, would you have your land with floods and droughts according to the will of God, or would you have no land at all?"

"Why, Doña Maria—what is this you ask? Surely a man would have the poorest land to none at all. Why, without land a man would starve, be it overrun with grasshoppers and full of stones to test his strength and patience."

Around him ran a murmur of approbation. "Verdad. He speaks truly. He answers for us all."

"Good!" replied Maria, rolling a cigarette. "Now answer me this: Of what good is this dam if you have no land to benefit?"

The hopeless bewilderment settled on their stolid, unlined faces. "But Señora!" spoke one solemnly. "We do not understand. We wish our land, of course. But why will not the dam be good for it?

"Fools! Burros!" spat out Maria. "Because if there is a dam you won't have any land! Will the dam be built in the empty air? No! It will be built on land. The water it will hold back will cover more land. The roads to it will require still more land. A lot of land, Señores. Whose land? Antonio's land; Guadalupe, your land; Trinidad's, Casimiro's, Berabe's—the land of you all. Now without land what will you care if there are no more floods and droughts? What will you do with the water? You will have no crops."

There was a moment of silence. "But Doña Maria!" It was a sharper-faced man who spoke. "Much land the dam will require. But not all the land in the valley. Is there not room for all, even with a dam?"

"True, Trinidad," she answered. "You think well but not far enough. Now think this far. You sell your land, your house, your barn. You and your wife, your children, are homeless, without land. But you have a bag of silver pesos. You walk down the road. You come to Policarpio's house.

" 'Policarpio,' you say, 'I have sold my land. Here is my

money. Let me buy a piece of your land to live on.'

"But Policarpio says, 'No, Trinidad. I have but enough for myself. Look, here are my six sons. When I die they must have land, too. I am sorry, amigo, but you see how it is.'

"So you walk down the road to the ranchito of Encarnacion, here. You would buy a piece of his land. Now Encarnacion is a wise man. He says, 'Trinidad, I cannot sell my land. This land is my mother, as it was my father's and my father's father's. What would I do without land in these changing times? I would be homeless, like you.'

"So you go to another house, to yet another. You go throughout the valley, and you can buy no land. Your woman has no place to make tortillas. Every mouthful of food you must buy. Your pesos dwindle. Will you leave this beautiful blue valley, your tierra, to return no more? Will you work on the railroad like a common labrador? You will be homeless as birds. You and your wife and children can roost in the pines. You can live on piñones, perhaps?"

In silence Trinidad stepped forth and faced the crowd. His face was red with anger. He beat a fist into his palm.

"Mother of God! So this is what you would do to me? You, Policarpio! You, Encarnacion! You pigs who would make a man homeless! Step forth if you dare and test the weight of this fist. See if I have forgotten the feel of the knife in my belt!"

"Gently, amigo!" purred Maria leaning out from the buggy to pluck his sleeve. "This is what would happen to each of you who would sell his land."

"Who says that I would sell my land? He lies!" shouted one from the back. "I will not sell my land. Not for silver. Not for gold. Not to any man here!"

"Not to any man here?" repeated Maria softly. "But there is no man here who wishes to buy it. Each has his own land like you. . . . Those who would buy it are not here. They are in town waiting for you to come to the meeting. On Sabado it is. To them give your answers, compadres. . . . Now adiós.

My own land waits. I must return to see that all is well."

It was not. Antonio de la Vega had not paid his taxes. So Maria called on her son, his wife, his son and his wife, their children. In the small dark room they crowded about her with coffee and homage. Maria sat back stiffly, keeping them at bay with thrusts of an angry gaze.

"Antonio, it makes three years you have not paid those taxes on your land. Do not lie. Now it is not a matter of eighteen pesos which I have ascertained. It is a graver matter. It is a matter of principle. You do not care for your land. Therefore I have come to tell you the land is no longer yours. Be off of it by the next sinking of the sun."

Indignation and protestation, pleas, tears—nothing availed against her. She drove them out with a set, stern face, a line of kinsfolk filing across the fields with blankets and pots to beg refuge of a neighbor.

To be sure, the next day they all drove contritely up to her hut, Antonio with eighteen borrowed dollars. Maria allowed him to pay his taxes and move back as before. But the lesson remained.

"See?" observed the neighbors. "Doña Maria keeps her own house in order. You should have seen how Antonio and his kinsfolk came to us. They were weeping and homeless. They had not a roof over their heads. Just as the wise Señora said. To any of us it might happen. Husband, are we owing any of this tax money on our land? Now you will understand, it is little but important. Muy importante! Verdad?"

To three races and four generations, through all its many names, it has been known simply as the beautiful blue valley. But to some men, one day each month, it is something more. It is a judicial district and a county seat.

At sunup the plaza begins to fill. By eight o'clock the hitching racks seem solid leather; the single dusty street is choked with wagons and horses; the exasperated honk of an automobile is less heeded than the honk of a stray goose pedaling through a forest of legs. Men crowd the cantinas and the sunny side of adobe walls. Squatting women cover the courthouse lawn. At ten the bells begin to ring.

It is true, there are three courthouses in Santa Gertrudes. One faces the inn, at the turn of the Guadalupita road. It is old as the memory of man. The floors sag, its huge vigas are dropping with the roof, the thick adobe walls are crumbling. Except, of course, the little patch of gray stone built into one side. "That," one hears, "was the wall of the calabozo. A good stone wall it took to hold El Tigre in his prime! His knife could cut through adobe as if it were cheese!"

Of the new one the people will be very proud when it is finished. It will resemble no building ever seen in the valley. It is cold and tidy as an algebraic equation, inelastic in line as law, modern as a stiff collar. It is a temple of that progress which recognizes no inherent qualities in different earths and races.

The second courthouse, chronologically, reflects a bit of both the others. It too was standard in its time, when a brown stone front portrayed the dull respectability of the gringo eighties. But life and time have mellowed its gaunt, stern body. Its hollowed stone steps hold rainwater. The dry air has cracked its woodwork. Cottonwood limbs hide its tin roof. Its brass spittoons spout stubs of hand-rolled cigarettes. A rag stuffs a crack in the front window. It, like the first, arouses the suspicion that even the Gilbraltar of law and order is not impregnable to the assault of justice.

To this one the people turn, lazily mount the steps to the courtroom. The cracking of piñones and the sucking of stick candy is in order. It is a show room big enough for all, though some must squat in the aisles. Cómo no? These are but more for the local políticos to impress.

But court raps its little hammer.

Jesús Alarcón is in the clutches of law. He was drunk that other Saturday night. He kept riding his horse up and down the flagstone portal of the old inn, and beating in the wooden shutters with his whip. Jesús Alarcón is fined five dollars. Señora Alarcón sobs buckets. She is going to get a beating tonight, because it is she who brings out from her rebozo the five dollars in a glass jar. God knows where she got them, but Jesús will want to know.

Jacinto Mondragon! You stole that white heifer from your neighbor Ismael Trujillo. You admit it. To Ismael Trujillo you will return that white heifer and give also that little Jersey calf of yours.

Ceferino Valdes! The case of El Estado y El Condado de Demora against Ceferino Valdes for stabbing with a knife the person of Mechor Santistevan. Mechor Santistevan may die, he may recover. The case is carried forward till God decides.

Maria del Valle. . . !

What! Mother of God! Can it be so? Our Maria? Doña Maria in the clutches of the law? In God's name, for what?

Feet shuffle. Heads crane forward. Consternation ripples through the room. Also eddies of satisfaction, people being what they are. Why, it was supposed that Doña Maria was greater than the law. And now. Look! She is no greater than the least.

Yes. Maria is sitting down in front like a captive hawk. Without doubt a hawk in its cage resembles little the one that flew so regally in freedom. Maria looks ragged, cramped and ugly. But still she is wild, wary and imperturbable. Her one tooth is clamped down indomitably on a cold cigarette. She might be sitting on her crag.

Don Teodosio sits besides her. It is he who feels the bars. He scrooges. His trembling hands pick at his sombrero.

"Maria del Valle! Remove that cigarette from your mouth. It is unseemly in a court of law."

Maria removes it to hide in her rebozo for later lighting. She does not look at the judge, but watches the político who shouts his charges at her.

"Yes! This witch of an old woman we have caused to be arrested. This very morning. In the very street outside. In her buggy she sat gathering men about her. Like flies about a honey jar. For what? To deceive, to ensnare with lies. Against the dam she talked. The good dam which is the will of all the good people of the valley. The very dam of which we will talk tonight in meeting. . . .Is it not so, old witch, traitress? Now you will pay!"

"Caramba! Burro! Fool!" answers Maria. "What man here has heard me say a word against the dam? I say build this dam. Build it I say! But find your own land to build it upon. Not ours. Build it in the air where all the promises of políticos are built! Is this not what I said? What man denies it?"

Bravo, Señora! Bravo, Doña Maria! Look! This captive hawk has ruffled her feathers. Watch out there, compadre, for that beak, those quick talons.

A small pandemonium breaks loose.

The judge raps for order with his wooden hammer. The room stills. Maria watches him now, respectfully.

He is tall and stooped, but he is younger than Teodosio. He is a good judge. Maria knows it. She had switched his little behind with a willow twig for stealing apples in the days before he went away to return a rich and learned abogado.

"What have you to say to this, Doña Maria? Rise, as is fitting, to address the court."

Time it takes Maria to unbend, straighten and try her stiff, rheumatic legs. And more to lasso the crowd with a look of cold contempt.

"The accusations are false, Don Eliseo . . . . "

" 'Your Honor,' please," interrupts the judge. "You address not me, but the robes of authority which cover me in this court."

"Your Honor," begins Maria again. "No man denies what I have said. You heard me ask. You heard silence answer."

"It is true, Señora, that you caused a great crowd to collect about you in the street this morning?"

"Your Honor Don Eliseo," says Maria slowly. "You

remember this old courthouse of ours. How its floors sag, its vigas drop with the roof, the walls crumble to rise no more? You observe this courthouse in which we stand. It is almost worn out. It can scarcely hang together. Now out this window you see the new courthouse soon to be ready. The third courthouse in this one valley. Pues. It too will wear out and crumble to dust. No doubt there will be more, and these too will sink back, outworn, to earth. It not that so?"

"The court questions Doña Maria, not Doña Maria the court, Señora," replies the good judge dryly.

"Pues! This then is what I observe." Maria glares round the room; she is not without a sense for the dramatic force of pause. "The steps and cries of men for justice have worn out even the wood and stone of the first courthouse. They have worn out the wood and stone of the second as well. They will wear out the third and all those to follow. The need of men for justice, Señor Judge, endures forever. Wood and stone cannot stand against it. Neither men, nor words, nor laws. Thus I say."

The good judge wipes his mouth. His hand hides a smile, but not his twinkling eyes. His raised hammer silences the angry políticos. He appears to consider both the wisdom of Doña Maria and the political expediency of the situation.

"Doña Maria. The court fines you two dollars for obstructing traffic on the main highway through town."

Doña Maria turns and stalks out of her cage without a word. Teodosio digs a dollar out of his pockets, borrows another, pays and hurries after her. They get into the buggy; Teodosio whips up the bony team.

"Mother of God! What a scene! We have defied not only the officials of the Compañía and the políticos, but the law itself. Before the learned Judge himself. And on the very day of the meeting, when all were there to see how resolutely we faced disgrace, destruction, a day in the calabozo or even a great fine. Santána, how they will talk about it! Our courage, our strength of will. Wait until the meeting tonight. Words will be hotter than chile seeds. . . . Ándale! . . . I must hurry back.

"Ah. . . . That Señor Judge, Don Eliseo," murmurs Doña Maria. "He whom I have switched for stealing apples not once but often. It shows what success and fame do to a man. With less fear of others' opinions he might have fined us only one peso or even none at all."

Usually by dusk the roads from Santa Gertrudes were crowded with people returning home from court. That Saturday they were empty: all had stayed to attend the meeting. Maria, facing from her crag the sun sinking behind the Sangre de Cristo, saw it all below her as she had always—as the beautiful blue valley.

But this was only its stark reality. All day it had been a judicial district. Tonight it was something else, a water district.

This latter premise the políticos duly expounded to the people in meeting. Behind the speakers sat two of the Mofres, some officials of the Compañía and several engineers all nodding agreement. Behind them on the wall hung great maps of the valley to further attest it.

The room was packed; townspeople had brought chairs and benches from home to fill the aisles. Bewilderment and resentment struggled with comprehension and acceptance on their dark simple faces.

The necessity of the dam and the benefits to be derived were being explained. Its location was pointed out to them on the large colored maps: there at the mouth of that cañon, here where the cliffs would provide anchorage. Up this way to it a new road, and through the valley still another. And behind it, a beautiful blue lake.

This lake people could understand. It sounded almost miraculous. There were claps and yells. Imagine, a lake where there had never been one before! As if God Himself would set it down. As easy as that!

During the applause Teodosio appeared. His battered

sombrero was askew, the fly of his rusty suit gaped open, his wrinkled cheeks were flushed pink as a babe's. "Ah, Don Teodosio! Doña Maria's Teodosio!" People respectfully huddled against the wall to let him pass. He staggered down the aisle and collapsed on the floor.

He was late, but not too late. Just as he had driven up in his buggy, he had met the good judge. His Honor had been much impressed with the wisdom of Doña Maria that morning. It had deeply pained him to fine his old friend. But alas! He spread his hands in mute eloquence. One of them came to rest on Teodosio's arm. It contained two silver dollars. Teodosio, himself an understanding man of years, pocketed them without a word.

"Law is law, and I uphold it," said the Judge. "But friendship is friendship, and I do not forget it. So to the wise Doña Maria, my good friend of years, deliver my profound respect and great esteem. Now come. I shall buy a drink. Not for myself who drinks no more and who must drive his máquina away this very night. For you. In memory of those days when we chased cows together through the thickets."

So Don Teodosio had sat with Don Eliseo and drunk his drink. It warmed his blood, stirred his tongue. He recalled those days—that day—"But I must go now, amigo," said the Judge rising. "Remember my message to Doña Maria. Also those two pesos. Forgive my mentioning them, but we are all forgetful."

"Of course, of course. I shall just remain here a moment in respectful silence while a great man leaves." And Teodosio had sat there in the dim and empty little cantina. Yet in that moment a friend had come and the two pesos had gone. They were not in this pocket nor in that. Nor would the bartender serve him another drink on credit. Teodosio unraveled his thoughts as he rose. He must go to the meeting. With something to tell Maria, and the Judge's message of esteem, perhaps he need not mention those two pesos.

So Teodosio sat on the floor listening. There were speakers

and interpreters, oratory and bombast, facts and figures.
Jesús! A man could not remember one. He squirmed about.

In the middle of a speech something happened to
Teodosio, it happens to the best of men at the worst of
times. He got up and struggled out through the packed mass
to the shadow of his buggy. The speaker glared at the
commotion, then resumed. In a moment Teodosio returned
to make another fuss. The people let him through respectfully as before, whispering to each other. "It is all right. It is
Don Teodosio. Without doubt Doña Maria waits outside in
her buggy. He has been out to tell her what is being said."

It had all been explained, the necessity of the dam and the
benefits the people will receive, where the dam will be and
the new roads, the amount of land it will all require. Now a
new speaker rose before them. "Such is the will of the good
people of the valley. You remember how you marked the
crosses on your votes? Well, the Government observes your
wishes, and is ready to build the dam. Now we are here in
this great meeting called by these your officials of this
illustrious water district. All the landowners of the valley. To
agree on a price for our land. For the dam must have land,
the roads, the lake. Some will need to sell. But at a fair price.
Is it not reasonable that we agree on one fair price for each?
What do you say, compadres? Shall we say four dollars an
acre for grazing land, the rocky mountain hillsides? And
thirty-five dollars an acre for the vegas, the fields in the
valley—the upper end where the dam will be, where the land
is not so rich?"

A thick silence eddied in the wake of his words. It was
stirred by the clatter of a chair, a noisy stumbling, the groan
of one with a foot trodden on. Teodosio was hurrying
outside again.

"He is hurrying out to tell Doña Maria!" the whisper
circulated. And when Teodosio came back in the people took
heart. "He says nothing. He sits with a bowed head. But look.
His face is grave. Doña Maria doesn't like it."

The men on the platform were having trouble. It was as if they were shouting down the throat of an empty cave, no one answered. "Come, come! You must agree on a proper price for your land. It is why you are here. Have you no speakers? Have you no opinions? Don Policarpio! Don Encarnacion. . . .Trinidad. . . .Casimiro. . . .Berabe! As land-owners, speak. You are among friends."

Feet shuffled. Eyes looked furtively at others. At last a man rose. "Four pesos is very little," he said. And then apologetically, "But I don't know how much is this a-cre. Still, perhaps I would not sell my best varas for four pesos. Where would I get more?" Thus he remembered Maria's words.

The ice was broken. More shouts, more men rising to their feet. Curiously, as if for confirmation, they all looked toward Don Teodosio who had risen and was holding to the back of a chair. His face was gray and sweaty; he was eyeing the back doors again like a man suddenly ill and contemplating a quick exit for relief.

It was the pose proper for the gravity of the situation. His refusal to answer shifted the responsibility to their own courage. His pale cheeks betokened fear that they had none. His posture of ready flight indicated his readiness to flee outside with news of their capitulation.

For behind him, presumably outside in her buggy, sat Maria—their common conscience, the invisible and invincible backbone of their solidarity.

It was a profound and significant moment: the moment that in all battles determines the tide of victory.

Teodosio turned, choked, excused himself.

At his first step, a man in the audience watching him shouted out in a great hoarse voice. "Policarpio! Encarnacion! Casimiro! Berabe! Do I speak for you? Do I speak for all of you, compadres?" He had jumped on his chair. His heavy muscular body seemed to rise out of his denim trousers, above his wide, brass-studded belt. He flung up an arm, pointed to Teodosio. "Don Teodosio! Do I speak for you?"

Teodosio's thin stumbling body stopped halfway up the aisle as if blown against a chair. He turned around, jerked up his head.

"Then!" shouted Trinidad at the speakers' stage. "Then, Señores! Listen well. We will not sell our land for four pesos nor for thirty-five. We will not sell our land for silver or for gold. We will not sell our land for any price!"

With an appealing look of bulging pride and indomitable stubbornness, he swung around to make sure that Teodosio had heard and would so inform Doña Maria.

Teodosio did hear a roar behind him, waved his scrawny arm, and weakly, hurriedly stumbled out to the nearest cottonwood. In a few moments he emerged from its shadow. His fly was still open, possibly wider. The lapels of his rusty coat he wiped off carelessly. Then, staggering a little, he made for his empty buggy and crawled into the seat.

A half hour later he was awakened. The pandemonium inside had burst into a bedlam. There were not only a hundred men shouting, but women screaming. There came the crash of a chair. Teodosio sat up and rubbed his eyes. The doors flew open. Out of the opening poured interlocked shadows cursing and yelling. They parted to let one stagger toward him. This shadow became a man with a shadow staining his shirt. Past Teodosio he staggered toward the cantina. Teodosio smelled blood and violence.

Hastily he laid a whip to his sleepy team, backed into the road, and turned for home.

Mother of God! What a meeting! There would be plenty of news for Doña Maria without mentioning those two pesos.

9

Maria tottered toward ninety.

She resembled an ancient Santo on one of Pierre Fortier's shelves except that her robes were threadbare and tattered black cotton instead of dusty motheaten silk. Under them her body had shrunk like seasoned wood. It was knotted and cramped from rheumatism. Her flesh was a dark, lifeless brown that had long lost its gelatinous sizing of boiled cow's horns and gypsum yeso, its paint of oxide and ochre mixed with egg yolk, its sheen of polished mutton tallow. Her white hair was thin and brittle as straw. Bent over, when erect, she posed a question mark supported by a cedar stick.

The fingers which clutched it were the prehensile talons of a hawk. But in her face still lived all the sorrow and fecundity, the passion and wild violence of the span of life measured by that human receptacle recognized by men as Doña Maria of the Valley. Its powerful and primitive features faceted them all. Her promontory beak of nose, high cheekbones and solid, cleft jaw jutted out from her dark wormwood face a savage, sad visage battered by time but still inviolable, a look that only an old Indian can encompass.

Her eyes refuted it all. They had gone dead. Their bright blackness was dulling to a smoky gray which only a brief flicker of the spirit behind could light up like milky opals. Perhaps they had been in-turned too long and deeply to focus readily on the surface life outside.

So when walking she began to poke ahead with her stick. It was a habit few observed. She received vistors while seated in front of her fire.

Maria, then, gave to all simply the aspect of a citadel beleaguered but still impregnable. She so regarded herself.

Yet, because the families of Gertrudes, Niña and Antonio anticipated her weakening blows with an axe, she was persuaded to accept the companionship of a grand-daughter.

"This Piedad of ours and yours," they lied, "is a good girl but a little wild through ignorance. She needs counseling. We wish you to take her, Doña Maria."

"I will accept her for the winter. To instruct her," Maria lied in turn.

Piedad's exercise book was a jag of frosty piñon and a rusty axe, her schoolmates a few shivering goat-ewes whose teats were torn by briars, her reward a bowl of porridge and a few leathery tortillas. She was small, sixteen, quick as a squirrel and more inquisitive. She was simpática. Maria liked her.

At night they crouched together before the fire. A white-bearded storm shook the hut and blew his frosty breath down the chimney. Piedad shivered, drew closer to Maria.

"Mi abuela, my grandmother Doña Maria," she asked, "why is it that children call that frightening boogie man whom none have ever seen 'El Abuelo'—a grandfather? Surely you frighten me not at all."

"My child," replied Maria. "To youth, age is incomprehensible. To ignorance, wisdom is frightening. So that El Abuelo having age represents the learning which the ignorant child fears. Now this is wrong. But even grownups have it. They possess learning and knowledge, and still fear the wisdom which they have not attained. We must all learn to be unafraid of the dark, the child of learning, the man of wisdom. Hence we shall all reach the true maturity which is eternal youth."

The fire writhed into a heap. Piedad threw on another stick. The flames uncoiled, rose up and shook like snakes. The resin rattled. The glare outlined pinkly the rows of goat and ram skulls on the rafters.

"Doña Maria," spoke the girl again, "it is said by all that by skulls and herbs you could read stars and weather, foretell good crops and misfortune, the future of man. Why is it you use them no more?"

Maria sighed. "Ay de mi, child! For many years I have ceased to read them. They were helpful in those days of my youth when like you I mistrusted the unseen trail ahead. It is true I had a knowledge of the signs and the events they portend. But not wisdom—the wisdom to perceive the future in each moment, in each stone and blade of grass. The past also.

"It is like this. A child looks at life as a wolf at the trail of his quarry. He has no sense of the past, only a hunger to devour the future. Thus, to pursue it with success, he soon stops and raises his head. He sniffs the wind. He observes the signs—even those on goat skulls. He listens to all the world around him.

"Now, you understand, he is at middle age. Having memory, he can see part of the trail behind him as well as the present he treads. But still the future winds unseen before him, up toward the cliff top shrouded in mist. He reaches it. Pues! That dreaded and hungered for future is no more than the present which resembles the past. They are all one. His fears were nought, his predictions useless.

"Entiende, muchacha? I will say it again for your simple ears.

"Life is a great white stone. You, a child, stare at it and see only one side. You walk slowly around it. You see other sides, each different in shape and pattern, rough or smooth. You are confused; you forget that it is the same great white stone. But finally you have walked around it, stare at all of it at once from the hillside above. Verdad! Then you see it: how it has many different sides and shapes and patterns, some smooth, some rough, but still the one great white stone: how all these sides merge into one another, indistinguishable: the past into the present, the present into the future, the future again into the past.

"Hola! They are all the same. With wisdom who knows one from the other? There is no time, which is but an illusion for imperfect eyes. There is only the complete, rounded moment, which contains all."

And Maria, with gray filmed eyes which saw more, clouded, than when they had been bright, reached blindly for her little sack of tobacco. "Ay de mi! Often I hear steps outside. I look up to see a man in the doorway. It might be Onesimo as he was called, a certain gringo soldado, Don Fulgencio himself, dead these many years. No! It would not surprise me if he were any of these. There are shapes of men less alive than shadows of men. So do even I confuse what has been and will be again with what is."

Thus in her wisdom she taught that winter the lessons which must be learned by each alone, and did not see the incomprehension in the girl's sleepy eyes.

But everyone else throughtout the valley paid her homage with extravagant praise as they plowed and sowed their fields again.

"Well, well, primo. We will have our land, thanks to Doña Maria. In our ignorance we voted for a dam. Then, with the Señora's wise advice, we refused land for it. Now there will be no dam. Ah, how black this loam is. How it smells!"

Maria had reached the peak of their regard, they almost called her Santa Maria. Yet she had no ears for their praise.

She heard only the gaping silence behind it—the lull before a storm. And far off, the faint rustle of that paper which was to build the dam.

To the families of Gertrudes, Niña and Antonio she said, "This Piedad of ours. She has learned the old ways. Let her leave me now. To go down into the valley and observe the new ways. Thus will her faith be strengthened."

To Piedad, alone, she said, "You have helped me well here, child. You can help me more, away. So leave this hut. Go down to the village. It is said that a criada is needed in the old inn. I would that you do the work."

Piedad was shocked. "A servant in a public inn? To strangers and gringos? It is not our way. We have always remained on our land, for better or worse, having no other master. What will happen to my modesty, my dignity, my pride?"

"As you know," went on Maria quietly, "that old inn has been empty for years, save on court days. Now it is full of gringos who are no doubt talking about this dam. Make their beds, serve their food and wash their dishes as instructed. But keep your ears open; you understand their tongue. Here!" She passed the girl an old square gold piece. "Buy yourself a horse. An old one but well breathed. From one of Antonio's neighbors. Ride up here to me weekly with news of what you hear. Teodosio is sick again. Besides, it will save his old buggy from falling apart and breaking your neck. Sabe? Listen to all, tell only me."

And Maria again drew back into the loneliness of her mountainside. She never left it.

The beautiful blue valley was changing swiftly. A new road had been built to one end from the city below. Another leading from the upper end over the high pass had been straightened and graded. The link between, through the valley, was filled in and tamped down so that the increasing automobiles would no longer stick in chuck holes and slide off slippery adobe into fences, cows. The new courthouse was finished and admired. Young people no longer danced gracefully to a few guitars the varsoviana, the vacquero and buckaroo. They hugged, squirmed and distorted their bodies to the blare of brass in dances enumerated to the old as "The Step of One" and "The Trot of the Fox"—though, to be sure, they still carried knives in their belts and razors in their coat pockets for ready use. Most of these dances took place a half mile up the road in a large new adobe intended for a later school gymnasium. It was called "La Casa de Gym."

"Who is this Señor Gym?" they asked.

Soon great saws, like steel beavers, leveled the row of old cottonwoods flanking the road past it. Only a few were left to stand back of a narrow cement walk built into town— drooping forlornly as if with immeasurable regret, not for their vanished companions which with them had shadowed the parade of hot, dusty, barefoot travelers with their bundles and children, the quarrels, seductions and rapes of a half-century, but for their own fate. They were the real tragedies; they had outlived their usefulness.

Still a red rooster, a line of geese, stray stock ambled down the village street deaf to honking cars. But the town had changed. Its pulse beat faster.

People generally were satisfied. Women learned to wear hats and squeaky shoes. A man had money to pay for them by working between seasons on a road gang. Children were taught English, though still the only school was not a State public school but one conducted behind the church by the Sisters of Loretto.

So they forgot the dam. They almost forgot Maria. Like all Saints she was left in her niche to be recalled in times of stress.

The long flagstone portal of the old inn faced Pierre Fortier's store across the road. Beside his front door he sat on his loading platform awaiting customers, jumping up to swat a fly and tally it, with a pencil stub on the wall. This appeared to be the gringo guests' only amusement as they waited for supper. Soon they drifted inside the inn.

It too was changing. The long bar now served as a hotel desk. Above it hung Kit Carson's brass kettle, a sword once worn by an officer at Fort Union, Jicarillo Indian baskets and Picuris pottery, old horse-hair lariats, faded French prints. The gambling room was a dining room, the green felt of tabletops replaced with checkered oilcloth. The dreary parlor still boasted the James Holstrom grand piano brought by the Colonel across the plains in an ox cart, with its fly-spotted scores of "After the Ball" and "Over the Garden Wall." An old tabouret was covered with a faded, velvet-lined Paisley shawl. On it stood a conch shell and a brass bound Bible. Over it, from the ceiling, hung an old round porcelain lamp painted with red flowers.

The men went out to their rooms, through a little square placita paved as the portál, its flagstones thrusting up from the roots of a giant locust, through a narrow zaguán into the large back garden flanked with a wing of the rambling building, sheds, and a crumbling adobe wall. Here, somewhere, were buried two men with their mules and a chest of gold, no longer dug for but remaining as ghosts to haunt the greed of credulous strangers.

In their dark narrow rooms the men washed in porcelain basins, combed their hair before crystallized glass framed in old tin. In all were large spool beds with feather mattresses, a great comoda for hanging clothes, a battered chest full of firewood for stove or fireplace. In one was an old rosewood cabinet covered with a doily and used as a dresser. No one lifted the lid to see the broken, rusty machinery inside, the bent crank and perforated music rolls of polkas, valses and French quadrilles.

But now through placita, zaguán and garden walked a young Mexican girl ringing a bell. The men came out, strolled lazily through the great greasy kitchen with its battered beams and roaring wood stove, and sat down in the dining room The girl lit lamps, served food.

The men were surveyors, engineers, laborers, clerks. They talked, an unceasing and vehement assault against the dusty silence and strange remoteness of their surroundings. The young criada was a part of both—a lithe, slim shadow in soft huaraches moving in and out among them without a word.

But once a week Piedad rode up to talk to Doña Maria.

"These gringos!" she said with a shrug. "They betray their ignorance daily. 'Hand me that gringo,' the woman will say in the kitchen when she wants the rolling pin. 'Señor Bolio', that is what we call a gringo to his very face. And he, being as ignorant of the idioma as of everything else, only laughs at the insult as if at a joke."

"These Anglo-Americans," corrected Maria, staring stonily across the clearing. "Yes, they are ignorant of some things as we Spanish-Americans are ignorant of others. So do not condemn them unjustly. When we both see all, then there will be no difference between us. There is little now. The good judge, was he not a ragged little chamaco? Is he not respected now by the Anglos perhaps more than by us? Simply because his eyes, through learning, have seen both ways."

This tolerance seemed unwarranted; she was getting old.

"But come, Piedad. What is it you hear?"

Week by week she heard, and so did everyone else. The Government was making a survey of the valley; old titles, queer old measurements were being investigated. Since the people could not agree on a price, the District Court had obtained appraisers to value their land. Finally there was a Court condemnation suit.

"What is this?" grumbled the people. "We have refused to sell our land, yet these strangers walk over our fields, they look at our papers. They say our land is worth this, now that. But that we will have to sell. No. We do not understand."

The day came when each received a little printed slip of paper advising him that his land had been appraised, condemned, and that he must move off.

Lines of men knotted in fields, in streets, before the bars. "Sacred Heart of Jesus! Get off your land, compadre. This is what it says to me, this paper. The impertinence! Do these gringos have a wish to test my strength and courage, the steel in my blade?"

"The same, compadre! It is exactly what my paper says according to Filadelphio Baca who can read. Come. Let us get another to read both papers at once."

They remembered Maria now. Daily they rode up the trail. "What does this mean, old mother? That I must get off my land! Carramba! Did we not follow your instructions? Come, Señora. We will not be betrayed."

"Señora! Good Doña Maria! To you we turn again in fear and ignorance. We do not wish to leave our land. Advise us again, Madre. For the love of God, Señora."

Maria sat bent over the fire, her warped bony hands clutching her stick, her filmy gray eyes unblinking as the papers were thrust under her nose. To threats and pleas alike she was obdurate. To all she made but one answer.

"Señor. . . . Señora. . . . Amigos. . . . Listen: I shall never see this new dam."

To her one day came the good judge, Don Eliseo. They met alone in her tiny hut, Maria crooked and bent, the Judge straight and brittle as an old pine, both wise, both wary.

"I am the Court and still your friend, Doña Maria. In me you see a personal man robed with the impersonal authority which he would not betray. So give me your hand and speak frankly. The truth is good for all, though for the weak it is often too strong to bear."

"You are always welcome, Don Eliseo," replied Maria sadly, "though it is you, cloaked with the robes of justice, who deals injustice to many."

"The dam cannot be stopped," went on the judge. "It is not a dam alone. It is new roads, new food and clothing, new customs to add to the old, education for all; it is the progress of the world which sweeps all nations, all valleys of men. No man can stop it, for it is of man himself.

"I tell you this, mi madre, for you are wise and understand. I tell you that you may tell the people, you who have a certain power over them beyond all others. Thus we may prevent fear and trouble, perhaps even bloodshed. Our people are quick to strike at what they do not understand."

"Speak on," assented Maria. "Say fully what you have come to say."

"The talk spreads," continued the Judge, carefully brushing specks of ash off his sleeve. "The talk of certain injustices. Now the Mofres, it is true, will be great gainers from the dam. They own the best land in the valley. They are members of the Compañía. Being rich they have bought much paper in the dam, and will thus derive a certain profit. Now this is not injustice. As you know, gold breeds gold. In every litter there is the stongest. And they have been sharper than most. That, Doña Maria, is inevitable.

"But this is untrue, that while the people will be paid thirty-five dollars an acre for their land, the Mofres will receive a hundred. True, they ask two hundred and yet pay taxes on fifty. But that is the custom, even with Pierre Fortier. I speak this truly: all people will receive equally what their land is worth. It is the Court, above all men, which has decided.

"Now all this is what I have come to say. And to ask you to say to our people to prevent fear and trouble, perhaps even bloodshed."

Maria laid down her stick, rolled and lighted a cigarette with a straw of popotito. She smoked it through deliberately, then again took up her stick.

"Don Eliseo. Two days ago the Mofres came to me—their enemy. They spoke like friends. They offered me gold for my land. Twice what the Court has said it is worth on paper. It was bribery; they knew my power. So I dismissed it as I dismissed them. I also dismiss and will not repeat what you have said about this talk of injustices and the Mofres. Those things, if they be true—and surely they must be, for I have heard them from you, my friend—must be corrected in talk by the Court itself. That is business. And I have nothing to do with business.

"Pues. Let us come to the truth that lies behind all this. What you say is no doubt so; it is not a dam. It is new roads, new customs, the progress of the world which sweeps all valleys of men in turn. You say I cannot stop it, that no man can stop it. I fear, Don Eliseo, that is true also. And yet I cannot bring myself to aid it."

Maria stopped, and rubbed her eyes before continuing.

"Let us consider my refusal to countenance my reason. I have opposed the dam, this progress. Now suppose I aid it. Pues! The people who trust me will jump the fence blindly as sheep to follow me. Or else they will turn upon me crying, 'Doña Maria! You have betrayed us,' and thus I will lose my dignity, their respect.

"That, good judge, is a selfish reason. I am above it. I am too old to crave men's acclaim and to fear their judgment.

"Let us consider it more fully.

"I do not oppose the dam, new customs, a new vision of life; I oppose nothing. But I uphold the old ways for they are good too. I awaken in men their love for their land for they are a people of the land. It is their faith. And so I place that faith above all the lesser benefits they might derive from that which would oppose it. Do you not see? I mistrust these benefits, they may prove temporal. But faith endures. It makes no promises, offers no rewards. It is whole and contains all.

"My friend, good judge, Don Eliseo. We move through time. But the moment comes when each must stop and assert that truth of which he is a part. It is not the whole truth, for man himself is yet incomplete. But it is the only truth he has. It is his integrity.

"For me, compadre, that moment has come. I see the good

in the future. I see the good in the past. But I am of my time, and must assert that which I am, and the faith behind it.

"So we must part. It is for you, being younger, to move on. I, being old, will stand for what I am.

"No. It will do you no good to talk further, Don Eliseo. Besides, I am tired and desire sleep. So go. But remember this, one can not do evil to save the good. So I will help you counsel peace if necessary. No more. Adiós, amigo."

Troubled with forebodings, Maria watched him cross the clearing. But where there had once been great pines and spruces there was now only a milky blur. She could only hear his receding footsteps.

At noon a big truck covered with a tarpaulin rumbled up into the valley from the railroad town on the plains below. It stopped in Santa Gertrudes before a tall adobe house with a peaked tin roof. A long wooden sign hung across the gable. On the porch pillars stuck paper posters: they were noticias containing the date when the people must be off their land.

A crowd of loiterers on foot and horse watched the driver unfasten and throw back the dusty covering, heave three large canvas sacks on the ground, then drag them inside the house. They followed to stand in a long line before a window in the tiny front office.

As the mail was distributed they came back out into the sunshine. Their hands held long envelopes which they slit open with calloused thumbs to reveal printed slips and long important-looking pieces of paper. Frowns beclouded their somber brown faces. They muttered to each other, stared angrily or dully at the papers in their hands. Then they began to crowd into stores and cantinas.

Next day Teodosio, Niña and Antonio with their families drove up to show Maria their own letters.

"Look! Here is one for you also, Madre. Open it. See if it is not from the Government like ours and all men's."

"Open it and speak!" Maria directed her granddaughter

testily. "You know I cannot read!"

Piedad obeyed. "It is as the others, Doña Maria. It is from the Government. It is to pay you for your land."

"I see no gold, nor silver either," grumbled Maria. "Am I a burro to be fooled with a piece of paper?"

"Los cheques. That is what they are," stated Teodosio oracularly as a mummy come to life. "It is what the gringos use for money nowadays. Now here is what is best to do; I have listened to the talk in town.

"We take these checks to a político who writes our names on them, we mark our crosses on them also. Then they are ours. Mother of God! A thousand pesos! We are rich! We can buy fat cows, new clothes, we can buy a new buggy, perhaps a little bottle to celebrate and to warm our old cold bones."

"Enough! Burro. Fool. Pig—and the sick one of a litter at that!" cried Maria. "What will you do with fat cows if you have no land? What will you do with a buggy, having no shed? Will new clothes be a roof over your head? And a bottle! Cristo Rey! If you had sucked more milk from a goat's teat when young, you would have no need for the strength of whisky to make you imagine you are alive.

"But tell me this wisdom of the street and cantina. Who would give you all these things for a piece of paper?"

"I see you do not understand," said Toedosio blandly. "We can take these checks to Los Mofres or Pierre Fortier. They will mark down the amount in their big books. Now when we need anything we go to the store and it is ours. Without money. With just a wish. Pues, as they say, this credit will last for years. Perhaps forever. I tell you we are rich!"

Maria nodded. "Yes. You are rich and homeless. So go, wander into the setting sun until you die. . . . But as you go, say this to all those who have also received these papers of money for their land. Listen well, Piedad, for you will go also to explain.

"Say this, 'Do not take your papers of money neither to

Los Mofres, to Pierre Fortier, nor to any store. For then these stores will have all your money; they will cheat you out of half and give you poor goods for the remainder.'

"Say also this, 'Do not sign your names or mark your crosses on these papers. Thus you will have to give up your land. By refusing, it may still be possible to keep your land.' Do you understand? Now go."

There were many who did not heed Maria's counsel. For there had come a bank to the valley. True, it was the same old, sound and unused adobe granary they had seen for years. But it had a new roof and iron bars for the windows. It looked strong and important. Two of the Mofres and Pierre Fortier were directors, and thus able to explain its new use and importance.

"You see, compadres, it is a big strong box like that in my oficina—strong against night and thieves. But big as a house and open for all of you. It is the kind they use in the city below. In it the Government and the Compañía will keep money to pay the men who build the dam. In it you may keep your own money, with proper instruction. Now to be true, it takes a man with knowledge to use it. But if it is your will to give me these checks of yours, I will get the money from the Government and put it in this bank for you. When you need anything—good shoes with glass buttons, fat meat, nails . . . for you know my tienda contains all of the best—then I will give it to you, and obtain the money for it from the bank at no trouble to yourselves. Sabe? Thus I assure you of safety against theives."

Yet there were those who neither gave their money to the stores nor to the bank to keep. They hid their checks in an old boot, in a box upon the rafters, in a buried glass jar. It was these to whom two Government men came with the sheriff and an interpreter.

"Look here!" they said sternly. "It is a month since you received your checks for your land, and yet you have not got your money from the Government. The Government knows this; it has its eye upon you. Now soon you will have to move off your land as directed long ago. Do you think to keep both money and land? So get your money quickly. You will need it to find new land, another house to live in."

To Maria they said this; and Teodosio, the families of Gertrudes, Niña and Antonio were there to listen also.

"Señores," answered Maria resolutely. "Here is my piece of paper. I will not accept it. The Government, the Presidente himself, knows better than to treat me thus. If you would take away my land, then give me silver, gold, money that I can see, feel the weight of in my hand, bite between my teeth. Here!" She tottered to a dark corner of her hut and brought back an old, warped, wooden box which she dropped on the floor at their feet.

"I must have this almur filled with silver pesos. Full and level with the top, Señores. It has always been the custom when selling and buying land. An almur—sometimes less, sometimes more—of silver for good land."

Vainly they threatened; Maria was obdurate.

They drew off together, outside the hut, to talk the gringo. "This old witch, this old fool!" explained the sheriff. "An almur is about a peck. I doubt if it would hold fifteen hundred silver dollars. And look. Her check is for twenty-two hundred dollars."

Vainly now they returned to plead; Maria was still obdurate.

"An almur of silver. Full and level with the top, Señores. It has always been the measure when selling and buying land. I will accept nothing else."

"Mother of God!" mumbled Teodosio when the men left. "It is you who are a fool. Money that you can see, feel the weight of in your hand, bite between your teeth! Our Guadalupana! You are getting too blind to see it. You have no teeth to bite it with. Besides that, where in this world nowadays can even the Government get a thousand silver pesos? To say nothing of those for us, for others also.We shall

all lose our land, our money and credit too."

Yet within a week the Government gringos returned. This time in a shiny new carro containing not only an interpreter and the Sheriff but a strange man from the city who held a shotgun across his lap. For Maria they filled the almur with silver; she herself blindly passed her wrinkled hand over the top to see that it was full according to custom. To Niña, Gertrudes and Teodosio they gave also little bags of silver for their share of land at the bottom of the cliffs and the pastures above, and to Antonio for his fields and vegas.

In the dim light of a candle in Maria's hut all sat in silence staring at the silver; Antonio dully; Niña and Gertrudes wonderingly; the primos and the children open-mouthed; and Teodosio, bent over, letting the coins trickle through his fingers to fall back with a gentle, metallic tinkle. "Madre de Dios!" he whispered. "I have lived to see it. Silver that flows through my fingers like water, like moonlight, without end. We are rich at last."

Maria stood up, crouching over her stick.

"It is nothing!" she said wearily. "So take it all. It is yours. Divide it equally among yourselves, and bury it against the hour of need. When the time comes that I leave you say simply, 'She had no land to bequeath to us. Only this silver which is meaningless without land.' Mark my words. In them lies your future and my directions to it."

Now to all the others the Government carro went in turn, to those who had heard of and followed Doña Maria's example, to Berabe and Trinidad, Policarpio, Encarnacion, Donaciano Romero, Quiteria Pacheco and the rest.

"Give us the check the Government sent you," they demanded of each. "Now make your mark upon this paper. There! Here is your bag of silver pesos. Now, Señor, the land is no longer yours. Be off it with all you own by the day set by those who come to build the dam."

This was the way it was. They hid their silver untouched or spent it according to their natures. Yet none of them could believe they would lose their land until the new road curved up into the valley.

A cluster of six dark red huts at Cañoncito stood before it. Two days later the fences were down; cows, horses, goats were loose in neighboring fields and lost in the hills; freed chickens and geese ran squawking to be flattened on the roadway; the houses and barns were heaps of smoking timbers and shattered adobe bricks. With all this disappeared Jesús Alarcón who had suffered a cracked skull under the weight of argument; he had been carted down to a hospital by a company truck.

The families fled shrieking to near vecinos, awaiting news.

It came straggling up the road; four barefoot childrn, Filadelphio and Señora Baca loaded down with pots and blankets, who had walked forty miles back to the valley after an absence of six weeks. Filadelphio was no longer the cocky rooster who had taken his family to the city to spend the money from his land. His new feathers were bedraggled. He was surly, and sat outside muttering to the men. Inside the house Señora Baca talked and shrieked between tears.

"God forgive us our sins, our pride and arrogance!" she wailed, not unconscious of the new power she had derived from them. "To the city we went, as you know, to live the life of the rich gringos; Filadelphio to work on the railroad and thus add more money to our riches. You see us now humbled to dust, groveling at your kind feet. Returned to the valley, our tierra, penniless and shamed, without friends. Ay de mi! You will be wise to turn us from your doors, we who have not had a tortilla since dawn. To refuse us your roof for this night. . . . What! An egg you are preparing? Cheese and tortillas, even coffee. . . ."

Soothed, she held up to all ears their six weeks in the city. A little house they had lived in. Near the railroad tracks. Where they could watch by day the wonderful trains, and hear the whistles and bells at night. Such a ferrocarril! It shook the house. Of wood it was. Pues. That was the trouble.

Of course, Filadelphio worked on the tracks. Very hard. A laborer. But money he got to buy canned peaches, canned tomatoes. You have tasted them? Seen those shiny cans with the beautiful pictures on them which can be pasted on the windows? Too, they walked the streets and saw the lights. All colors, burning at night as bright as day. They looked in the windows. Everything was in those windows. Mother of God! They went to the moving pictures. Not once. Many times. You have never seen a cinematografia? Well, that was the trouble.

It was true Filadelphio did not like his work. There was nothing of the good rich earth about it. It was true the Señora did not like her neighbors; they were very common. It was true the children were sick from eating too many peaches and tomatoes out of the shiny cans. Sí, that was the trouble.

"What was the trouble, amiga?"

"What trouble? Verdad! Are we not penniless, homeless, starved and shamed? Listen, as I have said, all this was the cause.

"Filadelphio did not like his work, so when he came home he was tired and cross. I did not like my neighbors, they were too busy to talk. The house was wood, not thick walls of adobe; it was always cold and required great fires. So we hid our bag of silver, and went to the cine. That's how it was.

"You see the night came when we returned to find our wooden house burned down. There was no bag of silver to be found in the ashes. Our riches, our future, were gone in the flutter of an eyelid, as quickly as the cine. so we have come here. We do not like the city. But where is there land for us now? What shall become of us?"

So the people began to mutter. Should they lose their money in the city like Filadelphio? Or remain in the valley to be cheated out of it by the Mofres, and have their heads cracked by the bolios like Jesús Alarcón? Meanwhile they retreated before the advancing road.

Unlike the old one which crawled along the side, following

the contour of the mountain wall, the new one cut straight up the valley. Nothing stood before it, neither fences, adobes, log corrals, nor fresh plowed fields, a hogback of slate, a deep arroyo. It was a furrow which split men's families, fields and hearts. Its geometrical precision taught the unteachable, that the shortest distance between two points is a straight line; this struck terror into their souls. And in its wake lumbered huge trucks and scrapers, winch-driven buckets and concrete mixers.

The French had come to the beautiful blue valley with steel traps; the Spaniards with their dead god nailed to a cross; the gringos with long emphatic rifles to punctuate their taciturnity. But now something greater than all gods, all persuaders of peoples, had entered the valley to entrap them. It was the Máquina of progress.

They began to turn against Maria. When they came to taunt her with failure she still answered with her curt phrase. "Courage, amigos. Meet fate with faith. I shall never see this dam!"

"No! You will not see it!" they shouted with derision, watching her wrinkled hand groping for a little tobacco sack. "You are going blind. Blind as well as toothless. Mother of God! So this is how you would betray us with your cunning words!"

Maria faced them like a rock. "Burros!" She spit at their feet. "You yourselves will never see this dam built."

Wonderingly they retreated down the trail.

"She has said it! Doña Maria has prophesied. We shall never see this dam built. Even now she says it," they muttered in confusion. To be answered by braver voices— "We did as she told us, and yet we are losing our land. Can you doubt it? Look at Jesús! Listen to Filadelphio! No! With all her wisdom and foreknowledge, she cannot stop this dam. She is a witch who has lost her power. She is nothing but an old woman!"

Their mutters against her were waves that left her spewed

up on her cliffs in silence. Their cunning against the Máquina robbed it nightly of shovels, monkey wrenches, air in tires; punctured gasoline tins, cut ropes; spit after receding footsteps. Their rage at the Mofres flamed up redly against the dark mountains and the skies of night.

Maria from her cliffs watched the roof of the store blaze up, the shed in back and two trees in front burn down before they could stop it. She heard shouts, a shot in the dark, a scream, and the clatter of a horse's hoofs splitting the night.

At morning she was still there. She was unable to see clearly the ashes below, but she could taste them on her tongue. They had the same taste as defeat.

Dawn-dusk lifted slowly as a curtain from the valley. Halfway up the mountainside the pulleys stuck. Darkness still shrouded the tips of tall pines and spruces. Below them, on the edge of a little clearing, stood a man with his head upraised above the noise of a waterfall; he thought he heard a sound. He was an engineer surveying the stream, up early for a trout for breakfast. Unwinding his line, he stared through the brush.

A small hut loomed clearer in the glade. From it as he waited an old crone hobbled out. She was naked and carried a long stick. Her flabby breasts hung dry and wrinkled, her ribs stuck out from skin brown and brittle as leather. In the breeze her long gray hair rippled. She shook all over.

Down to the stream she poked her way in the graying light. Her stick rapped on the stones like an early woodpecker overhead. The current in a pool she tested, then stepped bravely in. On her thin flanks she crouched in the icy water, then ducked deeper to full immersion. Great gasps shook here as she rose, groped for her stick, and slowly hobbled back across the clearing to her hut.

The watcher in the bushes shivered in his high boots and leather jacket. Then catching up his line, he stumbled hurriedly downstream out of sight.

Maria in her hut dressed shaking before a fire. For a long

time she sat huddled in a faded, burnt-orange blanket. The sun was high when she prepared tea and porridge. It was warm and bright when she sat down in the doorway to feed her birds. They chirped and squawked, ran, flew and pecked at her feet. A cottontail came up, ears erect, to sniffle the grain and hop lazily away.

It was the first day after the summer solstice. It was June and morning. Maria felt warm and well. She slipped readily into her morning nap.

Shortly after noon she called on her stick and strength to carry her up the trail to the cliff top. In an hour she was settled in her seat on the crag.

Vaguely she could distinguish the outlines of the valley below. She could smell the rich plowed fields, hear the chirp of a thousand blackbirds and the caw of crows. But when she stared above the mountain walls, at the sky above, she could see nothing but a milky gray mist. This was good; there were really a few tumultuous clouds rolling across the blue sky.

Near four o'clock rain fell, a short quick splatter on her head and blanket. Maria raised her face, let the drops run down her wrinkled cheeks. This was very good; it was what she had waited for. She felt baptized and refreshed.

By sunset she had poked her way back down the trail. By dusk she had eaten a bowl of posole, and drunk weak tea from the morning's leaves. Now, content, she rolled a cigarette and sat smoking before her fire.

It was el Día de San Juan de Bautista, and she had kept the faith.

On this day all the waters of the earth are blessed, the seas, the rivers and the ritos, the clear forest streams and all the muddy acequias meandering through the fields. So at break of day you must go down to the stream and bathe. Thus you will be immersed in the one living mystery, the waters of life blessed by St. John the Baptist, he who baptized the Cristo Himself.

For this day all week you have hoed your weeds, prepared

your fields that San Juan, the patron of waters, may favor your crops. Now this is the sign of his blessing to them and to you, who need equally the waters of life to grow and prosper, that at four o'clock, according to custom, it rains.

Water is like life. It is life. It permeates everything. The hand of God drops it at birth. It trickles down the snowy peaks, the little streams feed rito and acequia, the great rivers rush down to the sea. And the deep sea too feeds with mist and vapor that great blue lake of life unseen by us all, to be renewed again and ever.

What is life without water? What is life without faith? So all the waters of the earth are blessed, and all the flesh of the earth is permeated by its flow, and all the earth of the flesh is sanctified by faith.

For faith is not a concept. It is not a form. It is a baptism in the one living mystery of ever-flowing life, and it must be renewed as life itself is ever renewed.

This is the meaning of any dam, that it would obstruct the free flow of faith which renews and refreshes life and gives it its only meaning. It is self-enclosing. It means stagnation. It means death.

Faith is not to be dammed. It is not to be measured and meted out when timely. It must be free to penetrate every cell and germ of the whole. For it is the obstructed whole that finally bursts the dam, brings destruction and misery, swamps the temporal benefits of the past.

There are dams. There will be more. But all are temporal and unwhole. For they, like us, are spattered, swept and undercut by an unseen flow—a flow that is stronger than casual benefits, that never ceases to permeate and undermine our lesser faiths, and which can never be truly dammed.

10

There was no procession carrying San Ysidro to the cliff tops that May. Should he look down upon unplowed fields, an earth bare and bitter with change?

The people did not invoke the blessing of San Juan that June, nor congregate on the hillsides to watch it rain on his day according to custom. Of what use water when there were no weeded crops awaiting it?

Even the Corpus Cristi procession through the village, stopping at shrines of pine and spruce branches, was broken into segments and disrupted. Can people march four abreast chanting, kneel and pray in the road when huge trucks honk imperiously for passage and clog nose, throat and eyes with dust?

The earth was bare, water was disregarded, men's faith was broken. The Máquina of progress overrode them all.

From strange cities it came. Up from the plains of tall grass and short grass where the buffalo had rolled, and the long horns had tossed their square bows. Over arroyos and mesas into scrub oak and piñon, into pine and spruce. Through the forest it cut a swath; through the little mountain meadows where the deer had come down at night from the picachos to bound lazily over log fences and stand, ears up and unafraid, listening to the sound of squeaking wagon hubs. With iron girders it straddled the lower river. On white concrete and black asphalt it lumbered through the blood-red adobe of Buena Vista, the yellow clay of El Questo, the chocolate brown hillsides of La Cueva and the whitish talc near Romeros Corner. Into the beautiful blue valley it came.

These mountains would never echo the sound of a train, but the Máquina assaulted them with more than a far-off, thin and muted shriek. It clanged and jangled, bumped, rattled and banged. Past El Alto de Talco and El Alto de los Herreras, through Santa Gertrudes, Cañoncito, over La Corriera and Tramperas. To the tall jutting cliffs it rumbled ponderously, stopped and spread from wall to mountain wall.

Such a Máquina! It was iron and wood, steel and stone and concrete, bolts and long cables. It whistled, shrieked, snorted and clamored with blow and shout; it smelled of gasoline and crude oil, whisky and good coffee. It was terrible with power. It was wonderful with the new and strange. It was unreal.

So down the cañon trails rode people to watch it. From Luna and Lujan, from Vallecito, from Guadalupita and Turquillo and Lucero, from La Cañada del Carro. Men wary and flint-eyed, in hand-dressed leather vests, sitting their restless mounts. Women staring wonderingly from out of their cowls of black cotton. Children squatting transfixed in old box wagons.

"Ah, the Máquina of the dam, no less. It is worth traveling a day to see so strange a thing. Mira! I do not believe it!"

Of them all a bony little skeleton with white hair, and dressed in a greasy black suit with the fly sprung open, was the most bewildered and entranced. From morning till night he stalked the workings. His coat tail got caught in a winding cable reel. A wheelbarrow bumped him to splatter his shoes with concrete. A rising timber knocked off his little black hat.

"Jesus Christ! Get off that gangway, you old fool!"

"Hey there! You Teodosio! Watch out for this load!"

"God Almighty! You here again? Over there. Out of the way like I told you yesterday. I'll take you up in the next bucket but you gotta keep yer head down. Savvy?"

Don Teodosio smiled. He lifted his little hat politely. Out of his pocket he took a horse chestnut from the only tree in the valley, and presented it to the gang foreman. "Sí, Señor. Mil gracias. I have never seen such a thing before. I am overcome with awe."

There was this difference between them. Not that one was an ignorant, clumsy old man always in the way, and the others careful, efficient workers. But that they were childish slaves of the machine, their mother, while he was an individual unbroken to its will.

So this Máquina, this monster, labored to give birth to a dam there at the bottom of the tall cliffs which jut out to separate the crescent halves of the one long valley so beautiful and blue.

Steam shovels squatted in the fields, careful attendants to feed it. Great trucks rolled down and up the long macadam furrow bringing more supplies. The Mofres' little powerhouse was being built to warm and light it. Shops and a tool house became its nursery. A long mess hall and bunkhouse spewed nurses in dirty denim. The old inn held its doctors, filling with engineers and construction bosses and vapid wives to gawk at its souvenirs and bewail its lack of plumbing.

All waiting, like the people, to see born this child of progress, this new dam of the Máquina.

Ay de mi! Nature travails alone in the thicket, being hardy and not to be denied. But the machinery of progress needs much attention; it has no faith; anything may break down.

And all—strangers and people—watched anxiously the calendar and the posters which littered the valley walls. The people had been granted by court an extension of time before they must move off their land, and it was ebbing swiftly. . . .

Maria could now hardly walk. Yet each morning her stick, her grand-daughter and her own will carried her up the trail to the cliff top. She stayed all day—lying on her blanket under a pine and rousing from time to time to sit looking down into the valley. She was completely blind.

A dull rumble shook the hills, and then a clap of thunder.

"The great white-bellied clouds are gathering over the sierras?" she asked. "It will rain soon?"

"No, Abuela," replied Piedad. "The skies are stainless blue. It is the thunder of gunpowder. The men are blasting away that big rock across the valley."

Maria nodded. A moment later she asked, "And what do they today below us?"

"As yesterday and the day before that, Doña Maria. Those big máquinas are scooping up the fields. It is the sound of their great iron mouths you hear. As much earth they hold at once as the size of a house. And that clatter, Señora, followed by a whir. It is the carros swiftly hauling it away."

"I see, " said Maria soberly. "I see great iron gophers digging. I see great iron squirrels with their pouches full of dirt scampering away to come again. . . . Now that far-off whine and the sudden crashes of trees. Help me to see further, child."

"They are great round saws. Also run by small máquinas. They are clearing the hillside of trees."

"Like great shining gray beavers, no doubt."

"Sí, Señora," assented the girl listlessly. "Now come. It is time for your nap. I will rouse you when something strange happens. Then from the fire I shall make, you may have a cup of tea. It will make you strong for the walk home again."

"You are my good eyes, child. I will do as you say." And she lay down serenely in her faded, burnt-orange blanket.

Who knows she did not see aright this strange máquina?

We see in outer nature only that image which corresponds to our own inner nature.

But below her continued another unseen struggle. The people fighting time and gringos till the day when they must move off their land. Daily there were cracked heads and knife thrusts to be salved in court with patience and large fines, to be compensated for with days in the calabozo.

More and more men surlily rode up the trail to Doña Maria.

"Listen at that thunder of gunpowder; they are blowing up the hillside where I pastured my cows. Look at that patch of felled pines; I had been saving them for new vigas. Mother of God, Señora. Am I to stand by and see my land laid waste?"

"Peace," counseled Maria. "It is no longer yours. You have sold your land."

"Jesú Maria!" cried another. "That Campo Santo where our dead are buried. They are digging it up. They are carrying the old broken coffins, the gravestones, to unsanctified ground."

"Peace!" cautioned Maria. "The dead are dead. Remember your own living instead."

"This dam! You old witch! You said we would not see it built! Well what is going on? Are your ears deaf as your eyes are blind?"

"Enough! Fool! Has yet one stone been laid upon another? Has yet one timber been raised upon another? Remember what I say, you will not see this dam built."

And still the days thrust at them swiftly that day when they must move off their land. They became wild with fear and anger. They sharpened their knives. Their glances cut sharper.

"Look, old woman!" they shrieked. "Antonio's fields are a mess of machines; there is not space enough to harvest a turnip around his house. Niña and Teodosio's house is gone, their orchard cut down. They are living with neighbors. That is your land at the bottom of the cliffs, Señora. Where you lived a lifetime. Mother of God! Are you too old to love your land? Are you juiceless of feeling as a dried plum? Well let me tell you this, old fool of a woman. You won't even have this hut when the day comes. Now what do you think of that?"

"Good!" she replied calmly. "I almost starved a lifetime on that old piece of ground, to say nothing of Niña and Gertrudes and Teodosio. It was too full of rocks to escape with a plow. Now we have a good price for it. An almur of silver unspent, like yourselves. Peace. I counsel peace. Bury your knives with your silver. I will tell you when to use both."

Thus she counseled peace, remembering her promise to the good judge Don Eliseo.

The people went away angry. Their anger was fettered by their incomprehension of Maria, their incomprehension made fearful by her absolute disregard for her own fate. This was the secret of Maria's hold upon them, for it is complete freedom from self which alone makes possible complete creative power.

Yes! It was ununderstandable. For years Maria had fought this change and progress; she herself had aroused their love for their land, their fight against the dam. And now—Mother of God!

"It is as they say, Señora," confided Piedad alone with her on the cliffs. "You are not alone my grandmother. You are not only the oldest of the old among us. You are Doña Maria of the Valley. Men speak the name proudly to strangers. They speak of it as one speaks of the old ways, the wisdom of the hills, the manner of beasts and plants, the movement of stars and seasons, whom none know as you. Have you forgotten all this—though I beg you to forgive me if I remind you of those days when you were not quite so old? Have you forgotten, that you turn upon us?"

Maria lay back against the rock; her weathered face, tragic and timeless, seemed cut of a piece.

"No, child," she muttered softly through her gums. "I

have not forgotten. I have not turned upon you. I remember and thus give you the wisdom that rests in me.

"I see now that no man is greater than his time. I see now that nothing will stop this Máquina. So this I know, it is for each man and all peoples to become one with their defeat, and so rise above it. This dam has defeated me. I give in to it wholly. Thus I am free of it; it cannot touch me."

"But Teodosio, so old and bewildered and feeble, Niña and Gertrudes and Antonio, our good neighbors, our primos and compadres, all the good people—what will become of us all?"

"Enough, enough! Do I forget my people? Listen. You are of one time, like myself. But you have not exhausted its meaning, and so must belong to it awhile yet.

"For there are to your eyes two times. The time of the land, and the time of the machine, this great Máquina which replaces it. Now the time of the land has its faith, and we belong to it; it has taken long to root in our hearts, our blood has watered it. But the time of the Máquina has yet no faith, and so we must refute it.

"Do you see? No man can belong to a time until it has also a faith he can belong to. That is what our people do not like about this dam. It has no faith behind it to give it meaning. And so you must accept your own time which has a faith until the new time has also given rise to a faith, and you are ready for it.

"Pues. I myself am old. I have outgrown one time. I have superseded another. I shall soon die and be timeless. So it is only of you, of my people I think. Now plague me no more, for I am tired. I have thinking to do while I sleep.

"But meanwhile send me Antonio and Gertrudes' youngest son. And then the good judge. In my hands, as tools of my foresight, they will mark your future."

Piedad shook her head. "Have you forgotten, abuela? It makes two days that they came at your bidding, in secret, and with good horses. Now no one knows where they have gone or why."

"Pues," answered the old woman imperturbably. "When one sees into the future one may confuse the past and present. But send me the good judge, and tell him I would speak once more of a certain Don Fulgencio and the Sanchez you both know.

"Thus I shall insure my prophecy that you will never see this dam built. Now go."

So the days went. But Gertrudes' youngest son and Antonio did not return.

The day came; the day marked on the posters, in the hearts of all.

From the Court the carro came. To all the people in the valley who had been made to sell their land. In it were the sheriff with his gun worn outside his coat, a construction man in boots, a politician of the Compañía in patent leathers, and a stranger who carried a sawed-off shotgun.

The sheriff carried a paper of the Court. From it he read and spoke.

"Señora Quiteria Pacheco, the day has come. The day when you must be off your land. You have sold your land. You have received full payment for it. It makes a year and more that you have been living on land that is no longer yours. Now today you must be gone. With all your belongings. Before night."

Señora Quiteria Pacheco fell on her knees. She clasped her hands, the sheriff's knees. She wailed. "Madre mia! So it has come to this! That you would take away my land, my house! Where shall I go? To which of my three sons who have women of their own, with pots and kettles, blankets all needed to make a home? Who shall carry all my goods?"

The carro drove up the road to the ranchito of Fidencio Romaldo y Trujillo. The sheriff got out. A man walked out of the door to meet him, idly thumbing a long shining blade. At his heels stalked a shaggy mastiff. "Stop! Not one step more!" he cautioned lazily. "Or you come for trouble."

"I come with the paper of eviction, compadre," announced the sheriff kindly but firmly. "You have had a year or more to move out of your house by your own free will. Now, according to the law, we must help you."

The man spoke softly to his dog. It lunged forward, growling—to be met by a blast of the shotgun and roll over torn and bloody and still.

"I am sorry, my friend," said the sheriff. "I know how you loved your beast. But you see what lies behind me. It is the power of a law stronger and quicker than any knife. By nightfall be gone from your house, lest your own blood be as needlessly shed."

Through the valley the carro drove. To the house of Donaciano Romero, to the families of Santistevan, Espinoza and Montoya, to Policarpio, to Berabe, to Trinidad, to all the people who had been made to sell their land.

At each they were met with tears or dry stolidity, with noisy pleas or silent stubborn faces. "Mother of God!" shouted the sheriff now. "What have you been doing all year when you should have been buying new land, moving your houses, your furniture, your animals? Today is the last day. By nightfall you must be gone from your houses and land, though you pile your things beside the road. You have heard me. It is the law."

Late that afternoon the car drove in turning off the road and stopped; the lane was blocked with driven stakes. The four men got out, clambered through the fence, and walked slowly across the field. It was their last visit. The long, low adobe beside the dry acequia was that of Antonio de la Vega. But outside stood a crowd of men, Trinidad, Berabe, Policarpio, the men of the families of Montoya, Espinoza, Santistevan, Donaciano Romero, Fidencio Romaldo y Trujillo, the three sons of Quiteria Pacheco,—all the men who had been made to sell their land, all together, all at once. Behind them stood the women.

The four men stopped. One unslung his shotgun. Two

stepped behind him. One stepped forward and raised his hand.

"I would speak with Señor Antonio de la Vega."

"We have delivered your message," he was answered quietly. "The same you have delivered to us all. Do you not recognize us?"

"Just the same, I would speak with Antonio. It is proper according to law."

A woman pushed her way to the front of the crowd, spat. "Well enough you know my Antonio has been gone these two weeks or more with Gertrudes' youngest son. Where? Quien sabe? He is not here!"

"To you then, this same message. Be off your land by nightfall. It is the law. It is the last day."

The woman's black glance contemptuously whipped him where he stood. "It lacks no more than two hours before the sun sinks. Am I to move not only my own things, but those of Niña and Teodosio, and also Gertrudes' who have moved in with me? And to where?"

"To a kind neighbor's house—one whose land has not been sold," suggested the sheriff. "Surely friends will help. Perhaps one of them will sell you a piece of his land."

"There is no land to be bought in the valley. Would they lose their land like us?"

The crowd of men washed forward, like a wave, to engulf her. A tall paisano spoke.

"Pues. You see how it is. There is no land to be bought. We will not beg shelter like stray dogs. In one day we cannot change our lives. So here, all of us together, we wait the nightfall when you would drive us from our homes."

The sheriff rubbed his chin—a sign of weakness, no doubt. Like all men who shrink from might, he appealed to reason.

"I am distressed by your folly, friends. That you would accept money for your land, and yet not give up that which you have sold. That is not right, as well you know. But I am only an officer of the law. I do my duty as bidden.

"Now what man here doubts my courage? You saw me that day when alone I went after that old bear which had come down into the Campo Santo. In the cantinas you have seen me vanquish a borracho with drawn knives. Today also I will do my duty.

"There are forty of you with sticks and knives. My short gun will stop six of you. My compañero here will blow two of you to heaven or hell, according to your conscience. Which of you are these eight dead men? Suppose the rest of you kill us this day. Tomorrow is another day. Soldiers will come. They will destroy you all. Your children will not only have no land, they will have no fathers. What do your hearts, your minds, say to that?"

"We are waiting for the sun to set behind those peaks, compadre sheriff," came the soft, wary answer.

They waited. It was not the red flare of the sinking sun which came, but the thudding hoofs of a horse. Down the cañon road, up the lane, across the fields. To the crowd itself. A straggly-haired girl of seventeen on an old well-breathed mare. Piedad. Doña Maria's Piedad.

She slid off the bare-backed mare, looked sharply at the four and at the forty.

"It is exactly as the Señora foresaw!" she cried to all, sounding a little excited from shortage of breath. "The sheriff, the law, the Compañía and the gringo dam builders have come to put you off the land. There is trouble brewing. Is it not so?"

"What word does Doña Maria send?" gruffly enquired a spokesman of the forty. "Or are you here as a mere child to get in the way of serious business?"

"Let her speak," demanded the sheriff, as if she were the only straw left to clutch at weakly.

The girl spewed at him a curt and contemptuous message. "The Señora tells you to go away without trouble. To the court and tell the good judge he will be obeyed.

"To you," facing the crowd, she cried, "Doña Maria says

to get off your land. You have been too long at it already."

A murmur rose like wind in the pines—and as swiftly gone. No man listens to another's words. He listens only to that unheard but revealing voice of doubt, indecision and emptiness, of courage and faith and command, which is the voice of the one of many gods dwelling within us each. The people, then, did not listen to a seventeen-year-old, straggly-haired girl standing beside an unsaddled old mare. They listened helplessly to her who had been their master for a lifetime, to her faith and irreconcilable authority—to Doña Maria, whose voice was Piedad.

"She is blind but she saw you here," went on the girl, as if forgetting her commands but remembering clearly their contents. "She is weak but strong. So she commands you to peace. Move your things, this night, without fail, off your land. Anywhere! Into the vega, on the hillside, among the unfelled pines. Everything! Save all. You will need it for new homes. This she says. More too! Doña Maria will see to it that you have these new homes, new land. She is searching for them even now. Her own Antonio and Gertrudes' youngest son are her eyes, her hands, her feet. Now! Do you doubt?"

No. They did not doubt. Their credulity of the impossible sustained them. But they saw the shadows lengthen, felt the first faint stirring of the night breeze.

"My man is not here to help me. How can I move in an hour a life's home?" wailed Antonio's wife.

"How can I move this night? We have no wagon, no place to go?" grumbled another sullenly.

The man with a shotgun relaxed. The man of the Compañía talked swiftly to the sheriff who translated to all.

"The político of the Compañía says he will himself arrange with the law to give you not only this night, but another day. Is it not well?"

And now the construction chief murmured to the sheriff, who further translated.

"This ingeniero!" he shouted, slapping his companion on

190

the shoulder. "He is a friend also. He compliments you on your sagacity, and offers to help. Listen well!

"That vega there between the old road and the new one. There you can place your things. It is close to wood and water. More! To all those who have no wagons, no man, like the wife of Antonio here, he will send big bellied carros, his empty trucks and men to help them move. . . . But first to Donaciano Romeros', for that land he must use first and not delay his work."

More mumbling between the four; a faint flush had crept back into their cheeks. The tenseness drew out of the forty.

The sheriff raised his hand. He grinned happily. "Compadres! We are all friends. We will help one another. This very night let it begin! The ingeniero here, the big Jéfe, will send his men and trucks to help you move. Let the women build big fires and arrange their sleeping places. The político of the Compañía here, he will provide good coffee for all. It shall be a fiesta! We will all work and drink good coffee. Perhaps we can even find some fireworks to shoot off. Thus you shall move into the vega against the day when Doña Maria's Antonio and Gertrudes' youngest son return with news of your new land and new houses.

"Is it well? Are we all compadres? Shall we ourselves hasten away now to do all this? To tell the good judge, the law, as Doña Maria instructed?"

That night fires bloomed on the plain. Through the glow of leaping flames huge trucks rumbled like ghosts of buffalo, black shadows moved like ghosts of gone Comanches. Old comodas, great chests, heaped on the ground. Women spread feather beds and corn husk mattresses, cooked beans and slapped tortillas thin, sang children to sleep under the naked stars. Men cut wood, lugged water, unloaded and stacked furniture. The camp spread out. A great bivouac. At its edge nibbled tethered stock. A horse neighed to another; a cow bawled heavy with milk; a stray ewe blatted. From fire to fire crept mangy dogs to be beat away from cooking meat with stick and kick. The smell of coffee tinctured smoking cedar. There was whiskey too. So much the better: it made the fireworks seem more beautiful arching and breaking against the sky.

Maria up above saw and heard nothing of it all. She sat in her hut, ear cocked toward the cañon road down from the mountains.

Antonio and Gertrudes' youngest son had not yet returned.

The people waited homeless on the plain. Dust came in clouds, flies in swarms. Sand got in the sopa. Somebody fouled the sluggish stream. The sun beat down. The wind shook loose canvas roofs. It was no longer a fiesta. It was misery. The fourth day poured rain on stacked furniture, on sleeping mats, on food, on people. Then it was hell.

They did not grumble now. They sat with sullen lowered faces sharpening knives. When one did look up, it was toward the tall misted cliffs.

On the sixth day two horsemen sloshed down the cañon road to Maria's clearing. Their clothes were torn, their faces black with whiskers. Their eyes were bright.

"Doña Maria!" cried the younger, leaping from his mount. "We have found it! Our new valley. It is beautiful."

"It will do," supplemented the other. "I have looked at the land."

Maria roused from her blankets and rubbed her sightless eyes.

"To your people," she directed Piedad. "Antonio and Gertrudes' youngest son have returned. I would have them here to listen to what they have to say. . . . But first more wood on that fire. Put on coffee or tea, whatever there is. Your primos have wet clothes and dry tongues."

That evening they gathered in the clearing before Maria's hut. A single great fire had been lit to keep at bay the somber, pressing pines. As if oblivious of their presence,

Maria dozed in her doorway against Piedad's shoulder. She awoke with a start, groped for her stick and rapped loudly.

"For what do they wait? Let Gertrudes' youngest son talk first; he has spirit. Then Antonio. He can temper it with prudence."

The younger man had been talking already a half hour. To groups about him, his dark brown cheeks flushed rose; his eyes shone; his tongue, like a running stream, rolled obstacles out of their way. He gesticulated with enthusiasm.

"What a valley we have found!" he cried. "It is beautiful. It is untouched. It is ours."

A hidden little valley behind these mountains walls, up the Lucero. Rock walls enclosed it; it was dark and triste; it was high and cold. But a little stream ran through it. There was adobe for bricks, aspens for corrals and lattillas, pine and spruce for wood, for vigas, for lumber, for log corrals. A rutted road ran close; the one up the Lucero and the Coyote; six months of the year one could get down it by horse, perhaps with a wagon, for supplies.

This was what his hope painted to them all.

Antonio talked. He was old and cautious.

It was all true, what his compadre said, he acknowledged. But there was this to be said. To get into it with a wagon aspens must be cut down. For homes they must build their own, first of logs for this winter, till the adobes were made and hardened, the vigas cut and seasoned. There was no mill, the women would have to grind their own corn the old way. There was no stone. There were no neighbors—only that old Indian woman and her son who used to live at El Alto.

"But that is how we found it; we saw the smoke of their chimney," he said. "They have a cow, they have goats. The woods are yet full of game. Now listen. They have a corn milpa. The ears are small but well formed. I saw the earth. The leaf mold is a foot thick. It is rich. The land will do. Now compadres, consider all these things. It is a great step. Shall we make it?"

What was there to consider? When people are homeless they make homes of their desires. Hardships whet their appetite to enjoy frugality. So they began to build their dreams.

This land. It is untouched. It can be bought for four dollars an a-cre, according to the new measurement. The good judge will give us papers to it. Now we have unearthed our bags of silver pesos. They are yet unspent. It is not as if we are poor. We are rich. We can buy not only land; we can buy seed and nails, a new wagon, food to take with us. We shall have new homes and they shall be as before. No doubt when these neighbors of ours see our new valley they will also sell their land in this valley overrun with the Máquina, and come to join us. Verdad? What do you think of it, compadre? Does not your hand ache for the feel of a plow, an axe? And your old woman. Does she want a chimney and a place to hang her pots?

Maria began to mumble. She could not get up. The people crowded about her, squatted at her feet.

"What do you wait for?" she grumbled pettishly, punctuating her exasperation with the rap of her stick. "I have fought for life, and soon death conquers me. Do you doubt it? Pues! Am I fool to doubt it also? So I accept it calmly, and make ready to go to a better world.

"You have fought for your land, and now the dam has conquered you. Will you doubt it? Look at yourselves standing there homeless as stray dogs! So accept it calmly, like men, and make ready also to go to a better place.

"Where? Does an old blind woman have to show you? Mother of God! Your weakness overpowers my last strength! Antonio and Gerturdes' youngest son have told you; they will lead you. But I myself have seen it. As a young girl wandering with my goats long before you emerged from the womb. All they say is true. The land will do. Who confirms me? What man trailing a wounded deer has also seen this hidden little valley so close and yet so unknown? So go! You are a people of talk. Make action of your words, homes of your desires. It is I, Maria, who makes this her last wish for you all, her people."

They thronged down the hill leaving only Piedad with Maria's hand upon her arm.

'Momentito, child. To you only I have something to say. Let us go into the house. I grow cold quickly with dark."

When they were seated, the old woman stretched out on her blanket and smoking a cigarette, she said to the girl, "This Liandro who has been up here so often of late while you stayed with me. I have never seen him, but my ears know him well. While I slept you left me to hide in the bushes with him. Is it not so?

"No; do not catch your breath in shame, child. You will soon be a woman, as he a man. The spring of life rises in you both. It cannot be denied. It would be wrong of me to attempt to dam it. There is no dam but, in the end, is wrong; the dam of stone which would obstruct the flow of water, the dam of harsh morality which would retard too long the flow of life. But this flow must be sanctified by your faith in it or it is equally wrong. So dig in the earth below the bed—under that corner nearest this fire—and bring out the box you find."

In a moment the girl returned and placed the box in Maria's lap.

"No. Open it and receive in your lap the square pieces of gold it contains. They are few, all that I have left, but they are more precious than when I received them. Replace two only and bury the box as before. The rest are yours and this Liandro's. With them be man and woman together, buy a piece of land in this new valley, a wagon and the few things you will need. Thus your faith will be sanctified. If you would be husband and wife on paper first, so much the better. Though it will take a precious bit of your money for that lazy priest which might be better spent till you can afford it. For I would have you look at life more closely than at convention. For convention changes, but life endures. Your baptism in it, together, creates a faith that nothing alters. But you must accept that faith and never dam it.

"Now." She lay down weakly on the bed. "Leave me if you will. To ride down to this Liandro—if he does not wait already in the pines. Get ready to make your preparations. And be back again tomorrow: I need more wood as you know.....Now before you go, roll me some cigarettes. My hands shake. I waste half my good tobacco.

"Madre de Dios! I must be getting old!"

They were the defeated fleeing the advance of progress, their conqueror. Their failure brightened their eyes with longing, stiffened their backs to bear its burden. Long firm strides pushed regret behind them. Jokes leapt from their quivering lips. Hands strong to grapple the future waved tremblingly at the past. A cow tied to the back of a wagon set up an anguished bawling. They hooted it down with nervous laughter, and whipped their teams up the rutty cañon road. Their hearts clung to the poignant, their voices to the trivial.

"Mother of God! It makes three times that broken pot has fallen off, and yet she clambers down after it. . . . Hey there, Crescenciana! What will you carry in a cracked pot? It won't even hold your young one's water!"

"Mire! In the wagon ahead! Old Pedro still hangs on to his first wife's little sewing machine. Now he has no wife. Not even his third. Does he think to marry next the old Indian up there? Or will he sew curtains with it to hang between the pines?"

They plodded up the cañon. Old wagons squeaking under high loads, and drawn by straining horses. Horsemen riding ahead, and boys astride stray mules. Women walking to rest teams on the upgrade, and fading aside to squat in the brush like great hens under their black rebozos. And behind each group, a few head of stock: a lumbering cow with a calf trying to get at her swinging teats, a hobbled horse, some plodding sheep and blatting goats.

The steep cañon walls resounded more faintly their slow passage. The light, clean air, redolent with pine and spruce and rain-washed cedar, muffled their noisy cries. The swollen stream, pouring over the rocks at the rising trail, obliterated the shuffle of their anxious, plodding feet. Now only a magpie screamed from a branch that they were gone.

All morning they passed, a string of wagons, another.

"Adiós, our Señora! God go with you, Doña Maria!"

"It is as you said, wise old friend. We shall not see this dam built. But we will return when our houses are built. Sí, Señora! For you, wise old friend. It will not be long. . . ."

The old woman squatting against a rock on the hillside above them, stared blindly at the passing cavalcade. Her only answer to their last farewells was a sleepy nod and a thin, emaciated claw which lifted unsteadily and then fell back heavily into her lap. The sun poked through the fir above her and shone on hair gray and rumpled as the dead moss she leaned against. Her dirty black rebozo seemed streaked and rusty as the oxidized iron in the rock. She wiggled a bare toe in the green grass. A beetle crawled across her leg. A robin chirped.

It was these she really felt and answered. Men pass on, and their shadows follow. But the heaving earth and its blind vitality remains changeless and indestructible.

Near noon the last wagons stopped below her with their stock. People hastened up the trail.

"Doña Maria! Awake! It is us. La familia."

"Pues. I waited for your passing. You are late enough."

"Have you changed your mind, mi madre? Why do you not come? Now look. In the first wagon I myself drive my wife and children, Niña and hers, Gertrudes. In the second, Alfonso and Gertrudes' youngest son drive all our things. Never fear! We have lashed tight the good beds, the chairs, the cómodos, the stoves—all the big things are safely tied. The third is full of straw. It carries our pots and pans and

Santos, the breakables. In it sleeps Teodosio, and there is room for you. What do you say?"

"No, Antonio. Perhaps when you return in a week for another load I shall go. Perhaps not. I am not eager to travel. I like my own tierra."

Down in the third wagon a scarecrow sat up and rubbed his eyes. He shook off straw from his rusty black suit, put on his hat. Very stiffly he clambered out of the box. For some moments, back turned and legs spread, he stood contemplatively at the edge of the road. Then he squeaked slowly up the trail. His fly remained unbuttoned.

"Well, well, well," he chirped, blinking his rheumy eyes. "So Doña Maria still refuses to go. Sangre de Cristo! Look at me, Madre. I am old but courageous, weak but wise. They cannot get along without me. So I obey their will in this matter."

"Old?" rumbled Maria. "And courageous? Pues. You sick pig of a litter. You are too lazy to sit up. I have heard you need half the wagon to sleep in. And now you wish me beside you to listen to your snores!"

"Abuela, my grandmother, Doña Maria," begged Piedad. "With me you shall ride alone. In Don Teodosio's buggy which I drive. Will you believe it? It is able to travel again. Besides, Liandro drives our own wagon behind me. So we can see each other, not being together. I shall watch over you, and he over us both."

The old woman let her hand fall kindly and casually on the girl's head. Slyly she kicked the shin of Liandro beside her. But to the others she spoke harshly.

"Ándale! Get along with you! Has it ever been said that Maria did not know her own mind? Now go! You are long behind the others. But this I must say which comes to my mind, Antonio and Gertrudes' youngest son have staked their claims, there is not such need for hurry. So I would say let this Piedad and Liandro ahead of you in their wagon together lest all the good places be gone. Is there not an extra man among you to drive Teodosio's old buggy? Caramba! It might break down. It might shatter his kidneys. But that is more fitting than that a young bride be forced to ride alone in back."

"It shall be as you say," answered Antonio. "Now we go to return shortly. In your hut is wood and food. Is there enough?"

"Too much! Too much!" Maria cried irritably, sinking down on the grass. "Now go. My nap I shall take here now in the sun. Adiós. My blessings. Go with God."

Adiós, adiós, adiós. . . . They were gone.

"She is a wise one, no doubt," grumbled Teodosio as he was hoisted into his straw-filled wagon box. "We shall not see this dam built! Hah! She was right at that. But how about herself? True, she won't see it, but she can hear it, which is the same thing. Mother of God! You can hear that blasting from here. The trouble with her is that she has always known her own mind. And no one else. How can they? With all meanings in the same words. Pues. . . ."

The wagon rumbled up the hill, shaking. Don Teodosio, flat on his back, lay mumbling to himself under the clear blue sky. Soon his mumbling changed to grumbling; he had been refused a match.

"Let him smoke," whispered a wife to her husband on the front seat. "He is old and sick and weak. He ate nothing this morning. I fear his grave will be the first in our new valley. Jesús! Forgive me for saying it."

"No," replied he softly but sternly. "A cigarette in all that straw—God forbid! We would all be burned and buried before we got there even. . . . But what I fear, wife, is that Doña Maria herself—Did you observe how her knees shook, her hand trembled, her voice failed? She—No, I will not say it!"

He crossed himself quickly before shaking the reins again. So did the woman. They did not look back. Toward life the wagon rolled on, squeaking.

The lofty little valley was her cradle. The mountains rimmed her life. Clairvoyantly she saw in them now both her birth and death.

The sun was sinking behind the Sangre de Cristo. The snow-capped picachos were red as blood. This blood was ebbing swiftly. The peaks grew anemic; a slow pallor beclouded their faces. Then suddenly a strange effulgence lighted up the dusk—a light that came from nowhere, but as if from within, like a brief resurgence of life flickering up in a dying candle.

Maria rose shakily from her bed. She had slept all morning, again that afternoon. She had slept away the two days previously. There was still wood and a stack of twigs, food and tea, even a little coffee. Yet she had not eaten, nor did she eat now. She wasn't hungry. But she felt in good health and spirit—more resolute and cheerful than at any time of her life.

Quietly she toddled out of the hut. Life moved in a sustained adagio. The night breeze awoke in the pines. The little stream played its arpeggio on the rocks. A deer bounded over a string of logs, its quick hoofs striking a pizzacato. A few pigeons murmured on the roof. Two old goat ewes stalked across the glade and entered their corral.

Maria paused, breathing heavily on her stick. Noisy footsteps came up the trail through the brush, across the clearing. She could feel the warmth of a lantern when the two men stopped before her—men from the dam.

"You have come again?" she asked in a low clear voice.

"And for the same reason," one answered in good Spanish. "To tell you for the last time that you had better be gone. The blasting begins on the cliff tomorrow. There will be many men here to camp till the work is finished; it is a likely spot. All this will distress you, old woman. It may be dangerous, seeing that you are blind. Besides, you will be in the way.

"Now will you send word to your friends below to come

after you? I would take the message myself this night; I am going to the village. I am sorry, good old woman. But that is how it is."

"Yes, that is how it is," Maria replied in her low calm voice, without anxiety or regret. "My thanks, friend. You are considerate. It is a long walk here, after you have worked all day. . . . But I shall not burden you with a message. It is not necessary. By tomorrow I shall be gone."

She stood listening to their receding footsteps.

Slowly now she tottered to the corral and fed the two old ewes double measure. She did not shut the gate as she left, throwing the peeling aspen bars to keep out a chance coyote. She propped it open with heavy stones so they could get out at morning. Thus she did at the hen house for the three chickens that remained.

At the door of her hut she stopped, emptying a can of corn meal on the ground for the birds at dawn. She shut the door behind her as she did each night to keep out the evil spirits which fill the night air. Also, but for the first time in her life, she latched it.

The old woman was breathing heavily now, but no more than usually; such exertion always taxed her strength. Quietly a while she sat on the bed till her legs and arms ceased to shake. Then she got up and lit a candle. The one that stood before an old Santo in his niche, the one that she had cracked and mended a half century or more ago.

The pale guttering light made travesty of her putterings. She dug up the little box with its two remaining pieces of square gold, patted flat again the earthen floor. she smoothed the bed after removing from it the faded, striped, burnt-orange blanket.

Now with a little brush of popotito she swept the floor in a dark corner. Over it she pulled an old petate of woven tules. On this she lay down, and covered herself with the faded, burnt-orange blanket.

The candle stub burned steadily now, without a flicker.

Maria breathed steadily, without a gasp. It was as though she controlled both with an inner tranquillity, and the whole room hushed with her resolute assurance.

After a time something stirred beneath the blanket. Her wrinkled, scrawny hand emerged with the two square gold pieces. One each she placed carefully on her gray filmed eyes. They lay heavily, quietly, in the deep sockets between her high cheekbones and bony Indian nose. They pressed the calm assurance that they would not fall off.

These only were left her from a lifetime. There is nothing ever lost but unreal, evanescent images; nothing ever gained but a perception of the enduring reality behind them. This is difficult to learn. We must first learn that there is only one time, and that it contains all, eternally. Maria, having learned it, was content. She lay quiety, without moving.

A faint candle-lit darkness, and on the floor the shrouded shape of an old woman with gleaming spectacles of square gold. Like eyes of gold whose value could never be diminished by change, which could never be blinded by age and evil, or corroded by weather and misfortune. Steadily gleaming eyes that burned through time with a faith which could not be dammed, and with a gaze which saw neither the darkness of the day nor the brightness of the morrow, but behind these illusions the enduring reality that makes of one sunset a prelude to a sunrise brighter still.